HUNTED WOLF
A FOREVER MATES NOVELLA

TALA MOORE

CONTENTS

CHAPTER 1
LOGAN

"He'll see you now," the gravelly, smoke-tainted voice penetrates the sounds of the power tools and trucks that echo outside the trailer in the construction site. I look up and see a towering frame of a man, his head shaved clean. Our eyes meet and there comes the familiar heat as they connect.

He's one.

I'm the one to break the link because he isn't why I'm here. I've felt the eyes of four on me since I've arrived but it's inconsequential. They're just annoying insects in my way. I'll sooner stomp them beneath my boot before taking a step back in my journey. I exhale as I grip the arms of the chair I've been waiting in. My muscles and adrenaline beg me to leap out of it but I ignore them, gritting my teeth all the while. I know to give in is brash and short-sighted; it would be over too quickly and this is something I want to savor. I feel the chair's wood arms creak a little to my grip—better to displace it now than in the meeting. One final squeeze and the wave of adrenaline-fueled carelessness breaks. I rise with as much feigned nonchalance as I can muster.

Even though I'm vibrating with anticipation. Excitement.

The promise of revenge is now within reach. He's within reach.

I stand up straight and give the bald-headed man a small nod, signaling I'm ready for the meeting. He turns around and we begin our short journey to the office at the end of the industrial trailer. The fluorescent lights trigger something within me, an ancient memory from long ago. My heart races as the office comes closer and closer, my eyes narrowing, focusing me further into my tunnel of vision with every rush of new blood.

I've waited patiently for years, an entire decade to be here, at this moment. The towering man, who seems to be a giant walking in a dollhouse, passes through the portal to his boss, stepping to the side to let me enter as well.

The room goes quiet. Everything slows down. The pounding rush of blood behind my ears is the metronome of normalcy. The only thing I can latch onto until I force oxygen back into my lungs. He's sitting there, right there, talking on the phone like he doesn't know that he ruined my life.

Of course he doesn't know. He doesn't even know who I am.

But he will. He will.

The clicking of the phone being returned to its receiver brings me back to the present, standing in front of a desk in a cramped trailer with a bodyguard looming behind me. He finally looks up and sees me. The heat from the interaction lingers a bit longer than usual, only confirming what I already know.

He's the one.

He's the one I've been searching for. He has the same color hair as mine but his is pulled back into a tight knot at the back; the lights above betraying that it's been a few good days since he last washed. He gets up from his chair, not a remarkable frame, slight, but that usually means quick, unlike his second in command.

"Well you must be Logan..." he asks, extending his hand. His accent conveys a hint of Mississippian.

"Smith," I say, taking his outstretched palm into mine, reminding myself to keep things professional.

"Is it now?" he asks me with a tilt of his head, clearly not believing me.

"Best practice in my line of work if people think it is," I tell him, giving his hand a good shake.

He chuckles at my remark and releases our gentleman's greeting, but I know neither of us are fitting of the title.

"Something I can't relate to," he says, sitting back in his chair and motioning me to take the one in front of the desk. "In my line of work the family name carries weight, importance, status. I, Silas Beaumont, carry with me the legacy of all those who came before me."

I force a smile when all I'm thinking about is ripping this bastard's head off.

"Well it seems Beaumont Construction has been kind to you. Although, I must say, it's an unusual place to have a pack of werewolves working," I say nonchalantly, as if I was commenting on the weather.

Silas's smile fades slightly and he snaps his fingers towards the towering bodyguard behind me. The moving mountain squeezes by me and closes the door, leaving me and the fucker who destroyed the only one who ever gave a shit about me. The killer instinct that's served me well this last decade is clawing at the restraints I have in place, smelling the blood of the one who has wronged me so deeply.

"That's still something we like to keep just between our kind," Silas says. "I mean, we got some humans who work with us, you know, to help us blend in and not raise any suspicions.

And having this particular meeting at a construction site works to the house's advantage. The sounds of the tools and machinery keep prying ears from picking up on this conversation." Silas circles his finger in the air and then brings it to his ear.

"So this arrangement is something that you want to keep quiet from the rest of your pack?" I ask, anger simmering to the breaking point, but this is a dessert I need to be patient for despite my aching sweet tooth.

"You know how younger wolves can be, they take everything personally if it's not given to them," Silas returns to waving his hand, dismissing the matter as he leans back in his chair, establishing the pecking order in the room, an Alpha through and through.

"I actually don't, lone wolf remember? It's an advantage in my line of work."

"Your parents weren't part of a pack?"

The question is innocent enough, especially among our kind, but it triggers the animal inside me. My vision goes red and I see my mother laying in a hospital bed. My wolf hearing listening to the doctors tell me that there isn't much that they could do. The papery texture of her skin as I held onto her hands. The sad look in her eyes when she told me the truth about what landed us in our miserable, hard life.

The name of the son of a bitch who shunned her and made it so no pack would ever have us.

Silas Beaumont.

"Logan, you alright son?" The final word is the one that breaks me out of my fiery trance and I meet Silas's eyes again.

"There's someone that you want me to find?" I say, deciding to focus on the reason I'm here.

On my ticket to vengeance.

"Straight to the business then, I appreciate a man who

knows how to get to the point. Yes, there is someone that I'd like you to find. There's a nosey bitch who saw something that she shouldn't have." Silas opens a drawer in his desk and he pulls out a manilla envelope. "My boys got close to bringing her in but the bitch is slippery and smarter than we thought."

"How much?" I ask him, knowing that the price and target doesn't actually matter. This is just the last step before getting my revenge. Whoever I need to find will be the final piece of the puzzle; they're the only reason that I'm keeping my vengeful desires in check. They'll be the red herring to finally and truly put this monster in the ground and get justice for the woman who brought me into this unjust world.

One which will get a little better when I watch the last speck of life leave Silas Beaumont's eyes.

"A hundred and fifty thousand, brought back alive or you don't get a cent, understand me, son?"

My eyes go cold and icicles hang on every syllable as I tell him, "I always deliver, sir." He smiles at my seriousness, ignorant of the irony that he calls me son so flippantly. "As I told your bodyguard when he contacted me, I require twenty-five percent up front to cover expenses and costs accrued during retrieval."

Silas nods that he remembers and hands me the manilla folder. I can instantly feel the weight of it, knowing that my percentage is already in here. I pull back the tabs that keep the flap secure, the pinching feeling of their resistance against my fingers sending a thrill through me. After so many years, my body has been conditioned to relate this ritual of opening an envelope with food, shelter, survival. I glance inside and notice a Ziploc bag with two items sealed within it. I pluck the bag from the envelope, seeing a piece of jewelry attached to a chain and the white back of a small photograph. The necklace is the first thing that I grab and bring it to my nose.

The scent that hits me is like nothing I've ever smelled before. Honeysuckle dancing in the warm breeze of afternoon summer. My eyes flutter at the ecstasy, closing tightly as I try to get more distinct notes of the target's scent, while also trying not to reveal to Silas that something more is happening. I need to focus; I have to isolate as many scents as I can before my own smell begins to intrude on the piece.

I wonder what that would smell like?

I push the strange thought to the back of my mind and throw my hunting center into overdrive. I smell lavender, rosewater and a whisper of citrus but that's when I notice the thing that's driving my system with adrenaline and distracting me. Whoever this person is, they aren't mated. Although that's never mattered before. I let the chain tickle across my fingers as it's returned to the bag and then reached for the photo.

Hold it from the edges Logan, you don't want smudges, my mother's voice sounds in my mind.

With a simple turn of my wrist, I see the person who I'm going to be hunting. The one who will allow me to enact my decades-long revenge. The photo is an injustice to this young woman. Either from the shitty camera work or the fact that she's hiding under a hat and hoodie, I can't be sure, but I can tell that she's beautiful. The combination of seeing her along with inhaling her scent has my blood pumping.

Suddenly, the driving force that was revenge has been mixed with something else—desire. Desire to find this woman not just for my plan but to make her mine. The wolf inside of me has been launched into heat and I feel myself getting hard at the prospect of smelling her in person.

"Is that everything that you need, son?"

Will this fucker just shut up? I pack up the photo and reseal the manilla folder and get to my feet, teeth gritted. Silas stands as well and we share a final handshake. The feeling of his hand in mine makes my skin crawl.

"I'll be in touch soon. I'll make contact through your bodyguard. "

Just as I turn to leave, Silas jolts his hand forward and grips the cuff of my jacket. My reflexes are fast but so are his and I can't help but watch him rip the entire sleeve away from the shoulder stitching. I stumble back a couple steps towards the door, only to meet the firmness of the towering bodyguard, his frame filling up the now opened doorway.

"Logan, if you have any thought about taking that money and running, playing me for a limp-dick sucker; get rid of it. Because now..." Silas falls silent as he runs his nose over the sleeve of my jacket, inhaling it in a single breath. "I can find you and my pack will, too."

He pulls out an opened gallon Ziploc and deposits my sleeve into it.

This is what he must've been like all those years ago. The old shitstain hasn't changed much. It's the thought of him having done this to my mother that really brings my blood to the boiling point. I can feel the periphery of my vision growing blurry. The wolf within me is ripping apart my last threads of my self-control. He wants to go all Alpha and try to get me to bend...

I stop. He uses fear. He uses fear to get people to bend to him. That's what he must have used to break my mom and drive her away. The only problem is that I'm not afraid of him. With that realization, I get a grip on my anger, knowing that I have the advantage.

He doesn't have anything that can control me like he does with his pack. I'm free and I'll win.

The girl is my golden ticket to do that.

I give him a nod and feel the doorway open to me. I walk out of the god forsaken trailer as fast as I can and make a beeline to my car. I slam the door and make fast work of my belt, releasing the throbbing erection waiting for my attention. Even after squaring up and being threatened by an Alpha, my dick is still thinking about the girl.

What the fuck is wrong with me? Even as I think that, I make quick work of my hard-on, not needing much help with her scent still tap-dancing on my senses. My head falls back against the seat as pleasure climbs up my spine, my hand moving faster and faster. It must be the strain of seeing Silas, the excitement that my plan has finally come to fruition. I've never jacked off in a car like this.

Nor have I ever come so fast. I let out a guttural moan as the hot pleasure peaks, the smell of sweet honeysuckle so strong I can taste it. My hot spend seems to burn my hand, running down in thick ropes. I grab some napkins and wipe myself clean, throwing them towards the foot of the passenger seat, my growing trash pile. Good. I got that out of my system.

I look over to the manilla folder resting in the passenger seat and shake my head. I don't care what this girl has done to me so far. I can't let some piece of attractive ass distract me from what I've been working towards for a decade. She isn't a woman or even a person. She's a tool, nothing else.

She'll be the bargaining chip I'll use to get Silas Beaumont to confess to his crimes against me and my dead mother.

She'll be the nail I'll use to bury him.

With my renewed focus, I start my car as I chew on the bitterness that never leaves my mouth. Every bounty job starts the same. "And a hunting we will go."

I power out of the construction site parking lot.

This one will end the same. I never fail.

I always find my target.

CHAPTER 2

CASSIE

"**B**reathe Cassie. Just Breathe."

I clench my eyes shut, blocking out the horrible scene that surrounds me. I try to take a deep breath but the aromas of dried urine, feces and some other bodily fluids I'd prefer not to investigate yank me out of my failed attempt at meditation.

I open my eyes and see the sorry state of the truck stop bathroom I've found myself in. The actual smells aren't what's getting to me as I turn to face the single mirror barely lit from the dying fluorescent light—I have plenty of experience dealing with those aromas from time at school. School. The only thing that I'd always been good at, scary good at, almost freakishly good at.

But here I am in a truck-stop bathroom trying to meditate so I don't scream at the idiot staring back at me for ruining my life. I glare at my reflection and try to quell the discordant chocolate hue that's conquered the blonde waves I had a couple of days ago. The few stray streaks of blonde are the only remnants of the hair my mom gave me. The ache in my heart grows, but I shake off the thoughts of home and stare once again at the stranger in the mirror before me.

"Compartmentalize, remove emotion from the situation and assess what the next step is..." My concentration breaks from the percussion radiating from my stomach. "Fine, food is the next step." I turn away from the stranger in the mirror and grip the handle, giving myself one last scan to lock down my emotions.

With my newfound mental fortitude, I pull the door open and make my way to the food selection of the truck-stop. My hands reach into my front right jean pocket to count the remaining cash from my dwindling funds. Thirty-eight dollars —one twenty, one ten, one five and three ones. I have to keep the twenty and ten towards gas, the actual reason I had to pull into this armpit along the interstate.

My car gets twenty-two mpg. Gas is four ten per gallon which means my thirty allowance gets me seven point three gallons which translates to a hundred and sixty-one miles. That should be enough to get me to some town where I can start over or pick up a few shifts for some cash. That leaves eight dollars for something to eat. I quickly scan the food as I double check my math, even though I know I'm right and notice the food selection leaves a lot to be desired.

Beef jerky from two months ago and a slew of energy drinks that have the labels worn away are the more appetizing of the options, that is, until I see them. A basket with the sign that reads *fresh muffins, homemade, near the register*. I basically run, the rest of my body being pulled by the thundering hunger of my stomach until I land right in front of the basket. The flavor of what I was hoping would be mana delivered from the powers on high in my time of need is...banana.

Banana. Fury flows through me at the disappointment and somehow I feel that I'm owed restitution for such a terrible tease. Banana muffins are the lazy person's banana bread and my least favorite kind. My stomach growls again and that's when I notice the two for one special totaling three dollars. That means that my total remainder after this venture would be five dollars, an emergency fund of sorts, or rather the emergency fund of the actual emergency fund. I leaf through the bills extracting the one to total thirty-three dollars.

"Can I get thirty on five and two…banana muffins," I force myself to say it but my stomach's disgust is hardly disguised by the sound of my voice. The teller rings me up and takes the money so quickly and carelessly, I'm offended that he doesn't treat it with the shared reverence I do. But it's done and I need to go pump my car with my two banana muffins in hand.

I lean up against the side of the car as I fill up with gas, looking at the other travelers filling up their array of vehicles. I notice a truck with a dog poking his head out of a half-rolled down window. I smile almost out of instinct, but then the dog barks. The sound jolts through me, instantly sending my pulse into overdrive. My eyes shut and the memories come flooding back. One night. And the axis of my entire world tilted.

The night when I learned that I'd been walking around, blind to another world that had existed. Hidden just beneath the surface.

I was out for my nightly jog, something I've always done since high school. Something about it just clears my mind and allows me to fall asleep, emptying my brain of sorts. But not that night. I had to take a different path because of some construction, and this particular path was next to a large, wooded area.

The tracks were just starting to change on my running playlist. Such a short and seemingly insignificant second or two that changed everything. I heard noise—snarling and barks. I stopped for a moment and paused my music. The noises echoed amongst the trees again and something within me wanted to check it out.

The little voice in my head that says *Hey you're smart, should you really be doing this?* was completely silent. It always is when it matters most, but only in hindsight. I left the safe, grounding path of the pavement and ventured into the depths of the trees.

The sounds that had drawn me into the woods were getting louder with every step. The growls and barks increased in volume and frequency, telling me that there must have been at least a few dogs who were getting into a tussle.

It was only when I came around a tree from the high ground that I saw that it was a pack of wolves.

One was on the ground, with three others biting and tearing at it. The wolf tried to fight back but it was clearly weakening. It snapped as one came close, but even in the half-light, I could see its teeth were bloodstained. I tucked myself more closely behind the tree, sad to be watching such violence, even as I knew I needed to get out of here. Wild animals are dangerous.

There was a sharp bark, and I realized there stood a wolf merely observing, panting with excitement at another wolf being punished with such violence. The attacking wolves jumped back from their victim.

Some part of my brain reached into my memories of a zoology class, remembering wolf behavior. The attacking wolves were just the soldiers. The one who barked, it carried the authority, it was the pack leader, the Alpha.

A hand flew to my mouth to silence the gasp of terror as I watched the observing wolf transform into a naked man, as if it was a simple change of clothes. The pressure of my hand on my mouth increased, stifling a scream. This wasn't possible, biologically, or physically. Everything I knew tried to rectify the impossibility in front of me, but there was nothing. The world I had thought I knew was a facade, an ignorant illusion, I was an idiot.

My second glance found the wolf who was bleeding on the ground had also changed into a man, covered with bite wounds, nude and laying on the ground.

"I can still find him, Alpha. I just need another chance. Some more time," the man on the ground said crawling towards the Alpha, the other wolves growling with every inch he gained.

"Does it look like I give fucking second chances, pup?" the Alpha told him. "You failed to do what I hired you to do and these three right here, they're your replacements. Which means I gotta make sure they understand the terms of failing, of disappointing me." The Alpha scooped up something from the ground behind him and began closing in on the disgraced man, who had stopped in his tracks.

"Silas, don't, I can still be of use to you. Or I promise, I won't tell anyone about the baby."

Silas knelt down and grabbed the younger man by the roots of his long, bloody blonde hair. The glint of metal forced the moonlight to dance upon the quiet trunks of the witnessing trees.

"You just did."

The sound of a bullet ripping through skin and bone reverberated through the air. Silas looked at the other wolves in attendance and pointed the gun at the body, blood speckled across his face. "Now you know what's waiting for you if I don't get what I paid for."

The click of the gas pump reaching its paid limit yanks me out of my nightmare like an anchor securing me to the here and now. For a second, I just stand there trying to recover from the memory of that night. The night I learned that werewolves weren't just sexy, shirtless hunks in Hollywood but real, vicious, killers. Killers who are now looking for me and the reason that I need to get back in my car with my banana muffins and keep creating as much distance as I can.

I climb in, turning the keys in the ignition and smiled at the reliable and familiar roar of my car's engine. Just before I turn my wheel and continue on my journey, I look over and grab a muffin, beginning to unwrap it. One bite and I grimace at the flavor even as my stomach celebrates any kind of nutrition.

"You'd think that running for my life would at least get me a blueberry muffin," I say to myself before taking another bite and accelerating forward.

An hour passes and the sensation of normalcy begins to wrap around me. The wind blowing in my hair, my music playing from the speakers, I almost think that I'm just on an impromptu road trip like when I first turned sixteen.

That's the stubborn thing about reality. It always comes crashing in as the fantasy is getting good.

Freaking werewolves? How could werewolves actually exist and why were they so brutal? Though something keeps coming back to the forefront of my mind since that terrifying night, why is Silas so concerned about a baby? My brain doesn't like gaps. It likes to fill in empty spaces with logical explanations and it helps pass the time while I'm driving. What could be so important about a baby that Silas would kill that beaten wolf? Is he trying to find a baby or is the baby he's looking for all grown up?

My vision flicks from the open road to my right hand on the top of the steering-wheel. I can still feel it, even though it's almost been a week. The place where I wrap my mother's necklace around my wrist when I went for my nightly jog. In my haste to get away from the murder scene, I stepped on a twig and alerted the wolves to my presence, and while I ran away my necklace got caught on something and I lost it. I touch the area where the necklace resided and feel a few tears starting to prick at my eyes.

No necklace, and no blonde hair, my only reminder that I have a mom is an ache in my heart at never seeing her again.

Suddenly there's a clunking sound from the hood of my car and the steering-wheel starts to stiffen in my hands. I immediately look at the dashboard, not understanding what's happening. There it is, the illuminated orange light telling me that my gas tank is low, or in this case, empty.

That's impossible. My calculations were flawless. I had always been good at math. Can I not even trust in my own mind anymore?

With as much strength as I can muster, I slowly start to turn the wheel to get off the road and eventually come to a full stop. A glance in the rearview mirror suggests the tailpipe must have exploded with the cloud of white smoke pluming behind my car. I yell out a string of expletives and grip the door handle, needing to see if I can somehow come up with a solution to this problem.

I don't even think to check the side mirror in my haste to get out of the car and a split-second later, I wish I had. Climbing out, I see a sleek black SUV approaching. They flash their lights in the waning light of the afternoon. My brain is screaming at me to find something, anything that can be used as a weapon but there isn't anything within reach. There is a tire iron in the trunk but how would it look if I grabbed it before the person even got out of their car? My options are nonexistent at this point; I need help from whoever is willing to give it. The voice of self-preservation won't quiet down. *You have fucking werewolves after you! You can't let your guard down.*

As if an act of rebellion against my better senses, I wave to the driver of the car, signaling that I would appreciate their help. The car brakes to a stop and the door opens to reveal the driver.

"Please be a woman," I say to myself.

No such luck.

Out steps a tall man. He's wearing jeans, a light flannel, boots and a baseball cap. The boots are a dead-give away; he's a good ole country boy just helping a young lady out like his momma raised him to. This narrative I tell myself is convincing but the hair on the back of my neck stands at attention and that little voice in my head tells me to run.

He looks up, revealing his face hidden by the bill of the hat. My heart skips a beat, those dark brown eyes inviting me to melt into them. A shiver dances up my spine, examining the angular jawline speckled with a kiss of an approaching facial shadow. He flashes a smile and I feel myself angling towards him, almost like magnets falling into the field of attraction.

"You having car trouble?" he asks me as he picks up his pace to close the distance between us.

He approaches, assaulting my visual field with the fullness of his... sexiness. *Did I really just call a complete stranger sexy?* I place my hand on the trunk and take a step towards him, no longer able to fight the pull luring me closer to him.

Suddenly, that little voice in my head telling me to run for my life has finally gone quiet.

CHAPTER 3
LOGAN

"Like a lamb to slaughter," I mutter as I'm pulling off to the side of the road behind the car puffing out white smoke from the tailpipe. I didn't think she'd notice the steady stream leaving a trail behind her vehicle. I flash the lights to tell her I'm just some good Samaritan hoping to help out a damsel in distress. Quickly grab the stupid hat that I got a couple days ago just for this lure, I try to keep my heart rate under control.

This is the moment I've been hyper focusing on since Silas hired me.

After discovering Cassie's scent, it was easy enough to find her. Then everything else fell into place, leading me to this moment. I push back my hair so that it's nested securely under the hat, the bill shielding my face. Opening the door of the car and stepping out, I'm ready to play the part of some good country idiot who wouldn't hurt a fly.

The hair is the first thing that I notice. She's brunette now and I can smell the dyeing chemicals, even a few days old, from this distance. As I close the space between us, I ask if she's having car trouble. Only a yard separates us now and a breeze whips her hair forward from behind her shoulders. The scent, her true scent, rides the breeze and slams into me like a wall. My entire body reacts and I realize how much trouble I'm in. I thought hunting her dulled my affinity, but this is completely different.

I was given just a small taste and now I'm standing in front of the source.

My blood grows hot, adrenaline pumping my pulse to an alarming speed and my vision starts to get blurry. I thank myself for putting on the hat as it provides enough shade while I try to get my body back under my control.

Get your fucking shit together, Logan.

This girl is just a job. The job I've been working and wishing for as long as I can remember. She's the puzzle piece to Silas being killed, to getting revenge, to honoring my mother's death.

Bingo. Nothing like thinking about your dead mother to kill whatever is driving your libido.

"Yeah, I'm not exactly sure what happened," her voice is different than I expected, and it brings me back to the job at hand.

"Well, it looks like you have a leak in your tank. You've left a trail behind you," I reply, trying my best to sound charming and non-threatening. I watch her as she looks back at the car, inspecting the truth. I hide the smile pulling my lips, at puncturing a small hole in her tank while she was in the gas station. I think this might be my best snare since I started this bounty hunter career. "There was some construction a while back, do you think you hit a pothole or something?" I add, not wanting the growing silence to give her time to think she was working on a way to escape.

"Shit," she says, chewing her lip. "I'm sorry. It's just spent the last of my cash and was hoping that tank was getting me to the next town," she shares, resting her hands on the top of her head.

Another breeze whips past her and the siren song of her scent is chipping away at my resolve. I squeeze my hands at my sides, trying to get a handle on myself, again.

"Well, I think there's a motel just a ways up the road. I'm happy to drive you there where you can call a tow to take your car to the nearest mechanic," I suggest. "If you're comfortable with the idea that is."

She looks at me and I can see the wheels turning in her brain. She's weighing her options, only she doesn't have any. I saw to that at the gas station. She brings her hands down to her sides and gives a little sigh, acknowledging this is her only course of action.

"Thank you, that would be incredibly generous of you. Let me grab the rest of my things and lock everything up," she says before turning back towards her car to gather everything she probably owns.

"Take your time, I'll meet you in my car," I call out to her, heading back to my vehicle.

I'm suddenly aware of the new dampened area in my underwear, near my crotch. I need to focus and come up with the plan to lure Silas into a trap and kill him. I have the girl, the hardest part is over except for this attraction to her.

I get in the driver's seat and grab my phone resting in the center console. A quick flick of my finger and it's powered off. The two of us will be off the grid until I can come up with a more solid plan of killing Silas. The passenger door opens and her incredible scent floods the car. Why am I so fixated on this one woman? She's not even a wolf, at least she doesn't smell like one. There's one way to be sure.

She takes off her sunglasses and turns towards me.

"I'm Cassie by the way," she said, stretching out her hand.

I look directly into her eyes, never breaking contact while I take her hand into my own. My skin alights with electricity and I smell her pheromones pumping into overdrive. She feels it, too. Though I feel no heat behind my eyes. Nope, she definitely isn't a wolf which makes things much easier. She won't be outrunning me anytime soon.

"I'm Logan, nice to meet you, Cassie."

We unlock our hands and I turn towards the wheel, guiding my car back onto the empty highway and continuing onward with my plan for vengeance. Her smell is becoming suffocating in this tiny car.

"Do you usually make it a habit of picking up girls off the side of the road," she asks with a playful tone.

I look back and she has an eyebrow raised, mockingly. Is she already flirting with me?

"Well my mom raised me to be a gentleman, always help a woman in need, regardless of location. Plus I work in security, helping people is part of my makeup, I guess," I tell her and watch as she relaxes into the seat, angling herself towards me.

"Do you mind if I turn on the A/C?" she asks, nodding her head at me with a smile, a finger moving along the line of her collar, from her chest to her neck.

Thank god, I'm not sure how I would've turned it on without arousing suspicion.

"Please help yourself," I tell her.

She leans over the console to reach the knob on my side and in the outskirts of my vision I can see her cleavage teasing me from her tank-top. I look back to the road and try to take a few deep breaths as discreetly as possible; the stiffness in my jeans needing the majority of my attention.

The drive to the motel isn't an awkward one. I can tell she's someone who's always able to make friends, no matter where she goes. There is a lightness to her and when she laughs, it's like a choir of angels singing. We talk about everything from bad reality television, favorite foods to topics that go way over my head. It's very clear to me that she's smart, way smarter than most people I run into. It explains why she got as far as she has, any normal bounty hunter probably wouldn't have found her.

But I'm not normal and neither is the monster who is paying for her safe return.

Both of us get out of the car, parked in front of the office of the motel. My hands stretch towards the sky, the cooling air of the coming night tickling the exposed strip of my abdomen as my shirt slides upward with my arms. I can feel her eyes accessing my happy trail and a smile plays across my face. I know I've never been ugly and human women and some men find me attractive, but it still doesn't hurt to feel those wanton eyes upon me.

"I'm going to see if they can help me with calling a tow to the nearest mechanic," Cassie tells me from the other side of the car, tilting her head towards the clerk working the night shift.

"Okay, sounds good. I'm going to get a soda and wait for an update."

"You don't have to, Logan, I'm sure I can figure it out. You've already done more than enough to help me."

"Didn't you say that you spent the last of your cash on that now empty gas tank?" Cassie's face goes tight at the realization and that's when I put two and two together, she still has a credit card. *Fuck, this isn't good.* "You know what? Go see if you can get your car taken care of first and then we'll go from there." I shoot her a smile and a tip of my hat, which is driving me to drink for the entire drive.

Cassie smiles and nods before turning to walk into the office. I head over to the soda machine laying out my options. If she still has a credit card, then it would be like sending up a flare to Silas. He has the resources and motivation to track her cards. The only saving grace is that he'd probably have the mountain of flesh call me with the information. That's what will cause the problem. I'm supposed to be off the grid as well, while I figure out how to bargain Cassie. If he calls and I don't pick up or at least have my phone on, he'll send out his pack after throwing them my torn sleeve. I'm so close and she's trying to ruin everything. I pause for a moment standing in front of the soda machine. She's smart, that's why she's been using cash for so long. She knows what using a credit card means.

Shit.

What's my next move? I need to think of something fast. That's when I notice the option for a cherry soda on the soda machine. The solution's right in front of me and has been moving about in my jeans ever since I met her.

I need to seduce her.

It would be perfect. I could keep her from using her credit card on a room, I can dip into my cash for her tow and car getting fixed. I mean, tomorrow's Sunday and the mechanic won't be able to start working on the car till Monday. That at least gives me tonight and all of tomorrow to screw her brains out and have her dick-matized so that she won't want to leave. Sure, it isn't the most ethical play, but my business doesn't really deal in having a high moral code. Plus, it's not like I would struggle getting hard to bed her. It's been a while and I'm genuinely curious as to how it would feel with her. There's no denying I'm attracted to her and I can tell she feels something towards me.

"Find anything you like?"

I turn away from the soda machine to find Cassie appearing beside me while I was thinking about her underneath me. "No, not really. What did they say about the tow and car?" I ask, swallowing, my mouth having gone dry from my sexual fantasy.

"They can get a tow out tonight but the closest mechanic is ten miles up the road and they aren't open till Monday," she explains.

Check, the first two pieces are in place.

"Well, it is getting kind of late. I was thinking about getting a room for the night, could I get you one, too?"

Cassie shoots me a strange look, almost fearful. I might have been too bold in playing this hand so soon. Now comes the counter and course correcting if I need to. I can't let her out of my sight.

"You don't have to do that Logan, I'm sure I can swing something."

"Cassie, it's not a problem at all. I've been driving all day and definitely need to get some rest. I'm happy to have us stay in separate rooms till you get your car fixed," I say, trying to crank up the honey in my words to eleven.

Her face softens a little bit and she looks back to the office and then to me. "No, that's silly. If you're going to insist on staying the night, we could at least share a room. I mean, no need for you to spend more money after everything you've done."

Yes, the third piece falls into place. She'll be mine in a matter of hours.

"Alright, I'll go and get us checked in for the night." I give her a smile and walk towards the office.

I pay for the room in cash and they gave me the key to room 105.

I don't think I've ever looked forward to closing in on a job more.

C assie walks out of the bathroom with her hair still wet with a large t-shirt and boxers after taking a shower. She moves to the second double bed in the room I booked, even as I hoped we won't use it.

Even as I knew I'd have to make sure we don't.

She notices me looking and juts a hand on her hip. "Look, they're the best thing to wear at night. If you think women wear sexy lingerie to bed, you are such a guy."

I chuckle, but the sound quickly dies. Our eyes meet and hold, the air in the room thickening and heating. Cassie runs her tongue over her bottom lip, and the motion tugs at something primal within me.

She's mine.

I need to make her mine.

But if I move now, any semblance of self-control will snap. I won't be Logan the bounty hunter. I'll be Logan the wolf, giving into the desire that's burning far too hot to allow reason to live.

I can't lose my head. Not now. Not when I'm this close.

So I give her a crooked grin and walk into the bathroom. It's still steamy from her shower and the water is already hot after I turn the knob. I strip off my facade and step into the falling rain, trying to get a grip on myself.

The hot beads of water wash away the tension and aches that have been building up over the last few days of tracking Cassie. It's always like this hunting, the adrenaline and then crashing hard over and over until the job is done. What's more, the shower is a welcome distraction because it's the one place where her scent isn't dancing around me constantly. Yet even in this sanctuary, the damage is clear. I want her. I want to take her and make her bend to my will and desire. I want to hear her moaning my name as I show how well wolves can fuck.

I sigh, my erection growing from the mere thought of everything I want to do to Cassie. I close my eyes and turn the knob of the shower to cold and stand in the chilling onslaught till my dick is back to normal.

I can't afford to lose sight of what I'm doing.

Getting out of the shower, I wrap a towel around my waist. I slick the water from my hair and look at my hat laying on the floor. There's no point hiding anything. This is the risk of the gambit I'm about to play. I need to appear to be vulnerable and open so that I don't scare her off. I stand before the door to the room and take another minute to keep my mind focused.

This is just another part of the job and another step to ensure that Silas will come for her.

I grip the doorknob and open the door to the room. Cassie's standing at the foot of the bed closest to the bathroom. Just like that, the desire is back with the force of a tidal wave. How the fuck am I going to keep my head straight the moment I touch her?

Needing a little more time, I step out and try to walk around her but she grabs my arm and I turn to look at her. The familiar electricity of her touch shoots up my arm and my heart goes into overdrive. She pulls me closer to her until our bodies are facing each other, our eyes locked. Her eyes are green, just like mom's. Interesting how I didn't notice this sooner, but now there's no doubt about it.

A hand comes to cup the right side of my face and I find myself turning into it, as if I haven't been touched in years. I look at Cassie, who seems to have made a decision.

There's no point fighting this.

My hand travels past her cheek to cup the back of her neck,

pushing aside her still damp hair. Her eyes flutter at the sensation and she looks at me, something burning inside those emerald eyes.

"Logan," she whispers and I feel the knot of my towel struggling to hide my growing excitement at hearing my name on her lips. It sounds like a plea. Or a prayer.

I pull her closer and bend down, our lips just hovering a breath away from each other. "Cassie, you need to say it. I need to hear you say it," I tell her, whispering into her waiting mouth.

"Logan, I knew what I was doing when I agreed to share a room with you." Her hot breath coasts over my lips. "But I don't want to run from this. I want you. I don't know why or how but I do."

Her hands skim over my shoulders, grazing down my chest and finding their way to my waist where my towel is hanging on by a few threads. Heat follows her fingers like the tail of a comet.

I close the gap between us, both of our eyes closing as her hands make quick work to release my hard erection. My hand goes to the nape of her lower back and brings her closer. Her body pushes my hard-on into my stomach and the heat trapped between our two bodies makes it throb with anticipation. My other hand secures the curve of her ass and she leaps into my arms, knowing what I meant to do before I had a chance to convey it. Our tongues dance back and forth between our hungry kisses, starving for the passion exchanged with each shared breath.

The sensations, the smell of our desire, the sounds of our kisses, have my head spinning. Every cell wants to lose myself in whatever's been born with every touch and moan and gasp.

But I can't.

Trying to get myself under control, I throw Cassie onto the

bed and hear her yelp in surprise, but also in excitement. She grabs the hem of her t-shirt and brings it over her head, throwing it to the ground. The sight of her breasts, of that creamy skin begging to be claimed, has me bending down and griping the edges of her boxers. With my inner wolf breaking dangerously close to the surface, I almost tear them to ribbons taking them off.

Cassie lays there in front of me, breasts exposed, nipples standing firm and betraying her desire. There's nothing more I want to do than taste her. I snake my hands under her thighs and curl my fingers around her hips, securing my prize. Pulling her towards the edge of the bed, I drop to my knees, trailing kisses up her inner thighs towards the center of her pleasure. Her breath stutters. A flush of delicious red sweeps up her body. She wants this as much as I do.

Growling with satisfaction, I feast. The tip of my tongue dances around the swollen lips of her pussy, her cries of pleasure growing louder with my delicious torture. Moisture wets my chin as I continue to lick her into oblivion. I can feel the pre-come dripping off the head of my cock, begging to enter her. Her panting hastens and I feel her hips tilting towards my mouth. Her body is begging for my tongue to continue. The showcase of desire sends my dick into a throbbing fit.

Cassie's hands grip the still wet locks of my hair. "Logan," she moans restlessly. "I want you... I want you... I want you inside...now."

I find her looking down at me. I lick my lips, tasting her pleasure and my dick bounces in anticipation, no longer able to wait. I move upwards and Cassie releases her grip on my head, only to find my back, pulling me as close as she can get me.

Our eyes meet and everything seems to stop. I spit a bit of saliva into my fingers and then find the head of my cock, adding additional lubrication to the drips of pre-come. A silence hangs between us, the final prelude to the storm of sex awaiting us. Our eyes meet and Cassie gives me a final consensual nod. She bites her lip, anticipating what comes next, desire swimming in those deep green eyes.

With no other words or pleas, I guide my hard erection into Cassie and we both toss our heads back in response to the shock of pleasure.

My hips begin to thrust in and out and Cassie's legs wrap around my hips, meeting every thrust with equal hunger. We continue this dance, melting each other with every beat, moving as one while carnal need for release rises through us.

I grit my teeth as I try to think beyond this brand-new world Cassie is building around me.

All I need to do is not lose control.

Thrills radiate up and down my body as I meet Logan's thrusts, each one deeper than the last. He buries his face into the side of my neck and my fingers snake through his dark hair, pulling him closer. He's right there, clueless that kissing the side of my neck will send convulsions through my already taut body.

And it certainly does. I feel like I'm vibrating with pleasure, every nerve-ending alive in ways they never have before.

I open my eyes, seeing his bare neck as he thrusts into me. I turn and brush my tongue along his carotid, his quickening pulse meeting my onslaught, betraying how much he likes it. A moan escapes my lips as the curve of his erection twitches, releasing something deep within me. My hands migrate to his back, pulling him deeper than he's ever been, wanting this feeling of elation to last for as long as possible.

Logan shifts his weight and brings himself to his hands, holding himself up over me. In a rush of movement, he breaks away, pulling out. I gasp at the slap of emptiness and disappointment, wondering if the intense performance is already over. A muscle ticks in his jaw, as if he's under strain.

But no, Logan curls his fingers around my popliteal fossa, the back of the knee, and whips me around to lie on my stomach. In another quick motion, his grip is at my hips and he pulls me up to my hands and knees.

He enters me again and my arms threaten to give weight to the rush of endorphins coursing through my veins. I drop my face into the mattress, the sheets muffling my moan. The precipice I've been climbing to is close. So close. I push back with each thrust, now desperate to reach it.

Except his rhythm steadies, finding a pleasurable flow but it's just that, in and out. Something at the back of my brain nags me. It almost feels that Logan's just going through the motions, or holding back. His grip isn't tightening, just equal pressure. Not squeezing in response to what should be mind-blowing sex. I reach back and place a hand on his, gripping my hip.

"Stop," I tell him, my tone commanding and a little annoyed. He slides out of me, more gently this time and takes a step back from the bed. I scooch myself off and to my feet, my legs shaking a little at the new rush of blood returning to them.

I look up at Logan and he returns it with one of confusion, the one typical of a man who thought he was doing a great job.

I grip his arms at the grooves of his elbows and push him onto the bed. He lands, his erection making a slapping sound as it bounces back from hitting the hypogastric region of his torso. My gaze moves over him hungrily, registering the face and eyes that have made my body scream with desire. I approach him and he continues to watch me, wondering what I'm up to.

He doesn't flinch as I straddle him and bring a hand to his face, cupping his chin.

"You're not going to break me. So whatever is holding you back, deal with it after I've finished. Understand?"

A smile creeps across his features before nibbling his bottom lip. I reach between my thighs and grip his still hard penis, rubbing it against the lips of my vagina. His eyes flutter at the sensation and we both moan as I guide him into me, the deepest he's ever been.

I start to move my hips back and forth and electricity jolts right up my spine, crackling out like lightning.

I can't believe that I'm sleeping with someone that I just met a couple of hours ago but it feels right. Logan surrendering and letting me take the reins has made me feel protected. I'm in control now for the first time since that night in the park.

Safe.

The one feeling I didn't think I would ever experience again.

Logan tries to place his hands on my hips but I grab them. Our fingers curl around each other, gripping tightly. I lean forward and pin his hands to the sides of his head. Our eyes meet and that's when I see it. He wants this as much as I do, looking at me with something like reverence.

Is this what he's trying to hide?

My hips continue to move back and forth but I hasten the tempo. I'm approaching a dazzling peak, more than ready to shoot for the stars. Logan's breathing quickens, revealing he's also close to finishing.

"Cassie, I'm going to come," he says between his haggard breaths.

"So am I, don't stop," I tell him and he frees his hands from mine. He moves up and wraps his arm around the middle of my back, bringing me down with him, chest-to-chest. He holds me close as he quickly thrusts up into me at lightning-fast bursts.

"Come inside me," I tell him, my voice getting higher and higher as the tension within me is reaching its breaking point. I can't think about what I just said. He makes me feel safe; safe enough to do something impulsive and mildly stupid but that's for after.

Logan moans with a final thrust deep inside me and the

tension breaks. I moan at the waves crashing through me. My body sings at a frequency it's never known or that I've never been conscious of. Thighs, arms, and something within me convulses at the rush of oxytocin. Just when I think that I'm going to be swallowed whole by the sea of higher pleasure, weightlessness takes me. My body glides back to equilibrium, slowly. The descent is just as intense as the climb, I don't have to worry about movement. The pleasure seeps out of me gently, allowing my body to revel in what Logan had achieved. I feel the warmth of his semen filling me and it causes me to melt on top of him.

He stays within me but the tightness of his arms relaxes a little, not holding me down but just holding me. When I didn't think anything could make me feel more like my old self, I feel it.

Two soft lips lightly pressing the top of my head.

I lie there, a smile flitting across my face. My cheek rests in his smattering of chest hair as consciousness slips away.

I wake up groggy from the exertion to find myself on the fabric of the pillows. My eyes open fully, wondering where Logan has gone. With a simple turn to the other side of the bed, I find him looking at me, resting on the other pillow. The sheets hang over his hip, hiding the tool that had made me orgasm harder than any other guy before.

"You know some guys might be offended with a girl falling asleep after something like that," he tells me with a chuckle.

"How long was I out for?" I ask, thinking that it must've been a couple hours.

"Just thirty minutes. Glad you're satisfied with your service," Logan says, reaching over and tucking a stray lock of my hair behind my ear.

The tips of his fingers trail from my forehead to the arch of my ear and then continue along my jaw until they're beneath my chin. He leans over and briefly kisses me.

I know in that kiss that I can trust this man, even though the rational part of my brain is screaming to the contrary. He pulls away and lies on his back, one of his arms tucked up behind his head. A glance tells me that he's waiting for me to come to him. I sigh in defeat as I move beneath the sheet and rest my head on his muscled pecs. His arm comes down to secure me into place.

"Your car isn't getting fixed for a couple more days," Logan murmurs. "Maybe we can keep this going for a little while, even when it is."

I know he can only see the top of my head as my blissful smile fades. My reality comes crashing back to me, even in the arms of this trusted stranger. A couple days is already too long.

My lead over the werewolves after me is shrinking by the hour. This man has already done so much for me and all I've given him in return is the risk of getting caught in the crossfire of my life.

I take a deep breath and inhale his scent, knowing that I have a tough choice in front of me.

I either sneak away as soon as my car is fixed or I tell him the truth. The whole truth. He said he works in security, maybe he can actually help me.

The hardest thing will be trying to convince him about *what* is chasing me.

Fucking werewolves.

CHAPTER 5
LOGAN

I squint, chasing away the sleep that left my eyelids heavy. I wake up and see that I fell asleep facing the door. Something I've always done since being on my own. The feeling of the sheets gliding across my naked body alerts me to being fully awake. My feet swing to the side of the bed and find the awful motel carpet, dried and crunchy beneath my soles.

With one look back, the events of last night and the afternoon come flooding back to me in a whirl.

Cassie is laying on the other side of the bed. The sheet is in a clump near her chin as she rests in the crook of her right arm, hidden behind her now dark hair. I reach out to tuck back a loose strand of hair that hangs off the side of her nose.

I stop.

What the fuck is wrong with you, Logan? I didn't even realize what I was doing until my hand was mere inches away from her. I take a deep breath, and quickly find out why that was a bad idea.

The cocktail of our fucking still hangs in the air, her scent mixed with my own. It stirs something deep inside of me and I can't help myself. My dick stiffens at the aroma, wanting to add to it.

I rush to the bathroom as quietly as I can, not wanting to disturb Cassie from her slumber.

The thought of her looking at me, naked and delicious, is about to send me over the edge.

The door to the bathroom slides to a close with only a soft click before I turn to the sink and blast the cold water tap. One of the hand towels hangs from the rack, unused. I grab it and drown it in the torrent of freezing cold water, soaking it through. At the first shiver through my body, I take the towel and wrap it around my dick.

The cold splinters out from my throbbing cock to the rest of my body, forcing me to let out a small, strangled cry of discomfort and regret. I stand there embracing the shock and letting my breath return to normal as a minute ticks by. I'm careful not to move the towel. Any friction would be counterproductive. With another deep exhale, I release it and look down. It's bittersweet to find that the one part of my body that escaped my control has submitted once again.

I look in the mirror and move to place my hands on the counter.

"Get your fucking shit together, Logan. You fucked her to make sure she didn't ruin your plan. That's all this is... just fucking." I whisper to the reflection, seeing the words being spoken back to me. This is a job, no this is *the* job, the one that will lead to Silas's death. Cassie is just a tool. My grip tightens on the edge of the counter and I feel my knuckles cracking.

She isn't a tool.

I swear at the realization, turning away from the mirror and leaning against the counter, not flinching at the cool surface against my naked skin. She isn't a tool. She's something more now. My memories of last night come flooding back to me and I think how this could have possibly happened. The memory of her climbing on top of me and riding my cock until we both exploded with pleasure freezes at the forefront of my mind.

Her face, those eyes. That's when everything changed. When she forced me to look into her eyes. They're nice eyes but at that moment they were something more. An opening to her innermost being, her soul and she saw the same in mine.

With a blink of an eye, she made me hers.

A stinging sensation begins to bloom behind my eyes. My eyelids shut tightly at the pressure building. The heel of my palms fly to them and rub against the closed lids, trying to negate the pain with another source of pressure. Nothing is working. Flinging my hands down, I grip the edge of the counter again and move closer to the mirror. I count down from three, the sensation expanding to the entirety of the sockets. On three, I force open my eyes to inspect them in the mirror.

There's a sudden flash of a golden hue, shining from the rim of the iris. I watch as the gold starts to work its way towards my pupils until my eyes are pools of glowing gold dotted with a black center.

The glow fades and so too does the gold, leaving my eyes normal again, except forever changed.

I'm mated.

"Logan?" Cassie calls out from the other side of the door.

I reach over and flush the toilet, giving me an excuse for being in the bathroom so long. A minute of waiting later and pretending I'm washing my hands, the door slides open. I find Cassie dressed in her night clothes and sitting at the edge of the bed.

"We need to talk. I think you should put some pants on." Her eyes are fixed on mine and don't even stray to look at my naked body.

She has something serious to tell me.

I duck back into the bathroom and grab my jeans and slip them on before sitting across from Cassie at the edge of the bed. Her eyes are shifting from the floor to some random spot on the wall. Her fingers are playing with the edge of the t-shirt she's wearing. Her eyes close and her hands stop before she takes a deep breath.

"Cassie?" I ask but she just puts up a hand to silence me, still needing time for whatever she's about to say.

"Okay, what I'm about to tell you is going to sound insane but you need to just let me get it all out there before you call the crazy police, okay?"

I nod my agreement, still not sure if I'm allowed to start talking.

She gets up from the edge of the bed and paces in front of me. She stops on a dime and turns. "I'm on the run. I was in a park one night and saw something that I shouldn't have and it's been following me ever since." She draws in a shaky breath, and I wonder how much she's actually going to tell me. "I saw a murder, Logan…"

"Did you call the police?" I interrupt but she shoots me a glare, telling me that she isn't done and this isn't a question and answer forum. I swallow the lump in my throat and go quiet. *When was the last time someone was able to shut me up like that?*

"Like I said, I saw a murder and the ones who did it. But that isn't the crazy part." Cassie tugs on her t-shirt, then twists the material in her hands. "They were werewolves, Logan. I saw a pack of four wolves attack a lone wolf. And just when I was about to leave, I watched as two of them transformed into human beings. Werewolves are real, Logan. They're real and they're hunting me. That's why I don't have any cash and couldn't just call Triple A to help with my car." She stops and examines me.

I sit there, stock-still. She told me. I already knew everything she just disclosed, but she still told me. She trusts me, truly and utterly trusts me. The world fades away except for Cassie. I'm looking at her with my new, mated eyes. My wolf is growling deep within me as I realize what this means.

She's... Mine.

Everything's shifted. The moment I give her over to Silas she'll be killed. Yet one truth is now alive in my heart. Nothing will come to harm Cassie. She's gone from my prey to my prize. Even if I have to live my life knowing she'd never truly accept my being a wolf, it will be worth it to be with her.

"Logan? Are you going to say something?"

The world falls back into focus. My path forward is as clear as it was when my mother died. I stand from the edge of the bed and make my way over to her. She starts to take a step back, fear and unease in her eyes. My hand reaches out and snakes behind her back, holding her in place. I close the distance between us, knowing that there is no going back after this. Making love after the mating glow binds the wolf to his mate, forever.

The stories of my mom telling me about her mating glow ring through my brain. Those memories used to sicken me because of how well that mating glow served her...in squalor. But now, I have a semblance of understanding of my dead mother. She would've liked Cassie.

My free hand cups the right side of her face. She leans into my palm and my thumb brushes the top of her cheek. The fear and unease that were there melt away as she closes her eyes for a brief moment, appreciating my touch on her skin. She opens those beautiful eyes and looks deep into mine.

"I believe you, Cassie. Thank you for telling me. Listen to me when I tell you this." I step closer, wanting her to see the truth in my words. "I won't let anything happen to you. You and me, we're going to get through this. I promise you." I find myself meaning every word before I bend down to find her lips with my own. Her hands wrap around my naked torso and pull me close.

The wolf within grows excited and more protective with every breath we share. But with this increased protectiveness comes a higher vigilance that I haven't known. I can hear someone approaching our room from the outside. I peer at the door, still accepting Cassie's kisses. That's when I hear the scratches near the handle on the other side. I pull myself away and bring a finger to my lips when Cassie's about to protest.

My steps are slow and methodical as I approach the door, stretching out a hand. My wolf is the closest it's ever been to the surface, even closer than when I was facing Silas. I turn the lock on the door, freeing it from its frame. My fingers grip the handle, turn, trying to control my breathing but the wolf is just too agitated. It can sense the danger and knows that it must protect its mate. I swing open the door and in the few seconds before it's completely opened, my wolf is released.

My body condenses as bones move and muscles realign, the jeans I'm wearing sliding to the ground in a heap at my hind legs. A low growl is already climbing up my throat, my hackles at attention. No one is going to hurt Cassie.

A Shar-Pei dog pants in front of me, returning to all fours after standing against the door. The dog doesn't even growl but backs up and lays down, showing its submission. It understands that I'm not a wolf to be played with, especially with my mate so close by.

That's when I hear the scream.

CHAPTER 6

CASSIE

I can't believe it. Logan believes me and he's going to help me.

The touch of his thumb against my cheek as he holds me is all the proof I need. That almost foreign feeling of trust is creeping its way back to me and filling me up. The knowledge inflames the desire I feel for him. When he kisses me, I willingly melt into him. I've been so lonely with this knowledge and the burden of running for my life. Even though it's only been about a week, it feels like I've been out in the woods alone, stumbling through the trees.

Now, someone has come to protect me from the big bad wolf. I curl my arms around him to bring him closer, needing his kisses like air. His skin is hot beneath my touch, like holding it close to a radiator whistling to life. Muscles tense while in my embrace but I push past it. Like when we were having sex, I feel safe, secure, sheltered. He pulls his mouth away from mine and looks at the door. My hand comes up to caress his face, noticing in his eyes that he's actually a hundred miles away.

He moves out of my embrace and I turn towards him as he approaches the door, holding onto his wrist. He's even hotter there than his face—alarmingly warm. My medical brain can't compute how that's possible. How has his temperature spiked so quickly across his body? My hand falls away as he continues to approach the door, stalking it almost like an animal.

My body freezes like a statue, wondering who could be at the door. Is it the pack of werewolves who are hunting me? Have they found me because I stayed here for so long? These questions and more race through my mind as I watch Logan reach for the door and open it.

Everything moves in slow motion; my body getting ready for whatever nightmare is waiting on the other side.

Except it turns out it isn't behind the door.

In achingly slow detail, I watch as Logan, the man who was going to keep me safe from werewolves, became one.

His black hair and chiseled muscles morph into light gray fur, traces of white in the undercoat. A tail sprouts out of his tailbone, becoming erect, a signal for something I don't know. The jeans bundle on the ground, shedding his humanity with them.

Logan is gone and in his place is a wolf.

The growl is what brings me out of my slow-moving perspective. Reality collides like a train. My mouth opens but nothing comes. Fear chokes me. It keeps the ocean of adrenaline building behind it dammed up, waiting for the faintest crack to sweep through me .

He's with them. Everything is a lie.

The events of the last two days, my gas tank, picking me up, getting a room, play in my mind.

Seducing me.

The fear that was holding back my scream seeps into the rest of my body, wrapping its icy tendrils around every cell. Only one word enters my mind. One word to break this paralysis of betrayal.

Run.

Finally, the scream escaped my lips, reverberating through me and bouncing across the acoustics in the room. The dam breaks and the adrenaline that was waiting floods through me, overwhelming the coldness of fear. I break into a sprint, kneeing Logan, the wolf, into the door. It clacks against the wall from the collision but I don't hesitate. I run out into the world; its horrors a welcomed sight compared to what I just experienced. I notice I'm approaching the front office but come to realize that's a mistake. That road leads to questions and outsiders, which could lead to the wolves finding me.

Even though I know they're probably on their way, my brain has been in survival mode for too long. I break left and run away from the hotel into the emptiness of the night. The full moon provides enough light and I keep running.

There is nothing for miles.

My brain thinks back to how I thought being in the middle of nowhere would keep me safe. It puts distance between me and those who want me dead. Now the tables have turned. The isolation that's supposed to keep me safe has become a cage in which there's no escape. I don't dare turn my head to see how much distance I've put between me and the motel.

I don't need to.

It isn't the thumping of paws against the ground that tells me the wolf is behind me. It's the breathing. The exertion of the chase, of the hunt. I know only one thing after hearing that sound. He's gaining and he's going to catch me.

"Cassie."

That's it. Just one word and I turn back to look. Stupid. That one second of glancing back lowers my speed, giving him his chance. A naked Logan closes the last few feet between us, his arms stretched out. He skids to a stop as he grabs me by the shoulders and turns me around. The momentum from our speed pushes me backwards but he holds on tight.

We stop.

I'm still held in his grip. We're suspended in this moment until my senses come back to me. Pushing my feet into the ground, I bring my arms to my face and push outward with as much force as I can, adrenaline still fueling me. His arms come to his sides and he tries to step closer. Without even thinking about it, I slap him across the face. There's a faint sting at the palm of my hand after the impact but it's barely noticeable because of how amped I am.

He turns his gaze back to me, his jaw tight, and tries to approach again. I swing with my other hand but he catches it by my wrist, holding it like a vice. I try for another hit with my free hand, only to be met with the same result. I shift my weight and lean into a hard kick right to his side. His eyes close briefly at the blow and then he looks back at me.

The pale moonlight seems to accentuate the pallor of his skin and its stark contrast to his onyx-like hair. He's beautiful, but he's also a liar. In one fluid motion, he moves his arms so I'm constricted by my own with my back to his chest. I feel the rising and falling of his bare chest against me and then something else, poking up against the curve of my ass.

"Are you fucking kidding me? You have a hard-on? Now?" I ask him, my jaw dropping in horror.

"You made me chase you," he whispers in my ear.

I can feel the smile across his lips.

That's it, I need to get out of here. I thrust my hips forward and spring back, smashing into his dick with all the anger I'm feeling. That does the trick and I'm released from his grip. I guess werewolves are more man than wolf, after all. I whip around and find Logan squatting down and breathing hard from the impact.

"You were sent to kill me, weren't you," I scream at him.

It's not a question and his silence only confirms it. I lose my patience and go up to the bastard, slapping him while he's still crouched down. He just sits there, taking one hit after the other. With every smack and second of standing over him, the adrenaline leaves my system. The pain from my onslaught seeps deep into my hands and I finally stop. Sobs erupt from me and tears leave tracks on my cheeks.

"What am I to you, Logan?" I ask, realizing that might not even be his actual name. I turn my back to him, not wanting him to see me cry, even though he can hear it. But between my sobs for something that couldn't have been real, I hear him say one word.

"Everything."

I go quiet and look back. "What?" I ask, venom dripping from the single syllable.

"You're everything," he says, looking up to finally meet my gaze. There's a hint of desperation in his voice. He stands up, never breaking eye contact. "Cassie, you have every right to be pissed at me, hate me even. But please, don't run away. I meant what I said. I really did. Please. Please come back with me. Give me a chance to explain. I'll answer every question you have. At least listen to what I have to say before you decide what to do next."

He stands there after his speech and looks at me with something new in his eyes. He looks afraid. What's he afraid of? That scared look tugs at my heart and I find myself being pulled to him. It doesn't make any sense, but I think about cradling him in my arms with that look of pleading.

"Okay," I say, surprising even myself.

He looks to me with equal surprise but gives a nod like he did moments before in the room. I cross my arms as I begin to walk back to the motel, moving away when he tries to lead me with a hand.

"I have to turn back until we get into the room," he tells me.

"Are you serious?"

"Yeah, can't have a naked guy walking around the motel, people would call the cops."

"But a gray wolf is easier to explain?"

"It's easier to sneak around as a wolf. Most people just think I'm a dog or something," he explains as we continue to get closer to the motel. He shifts back into his wolf form and walks alongside me, glancing upwards to make sure I'm not running away.

I keep walking, keeping my gaze straight ahead. I refuse to look longer than I need to at a wolf who's also a man.

Don't let yourself be fooled, Cassie. You need to get back control of the situation. I'm stranded in the middle of nowhere with no money or car. How the fuck am I going to get control back? The answer comes to me like a lightning bolt.

The jeans.

He hasn't worn them since last night when we arrived. He had to go get them from the bathroom when I told him about my situation. His keys and wallet were probably in the pockets. Even if they weren't, then they'd be in his pile of clothes in the bathroom. If I can find his wallet and keys, I'll have a way out of here and his money to spend as I need. I'll pretend to listen to whatever fantasy he's going to peddle and then say I need to get some air. That'll be my moment and the end of dealing with Liar Logan.

We get to the still opened door of our room and he walks in first, past his jeans. I walk in quickly after him while he shifts back into his human form. I close the door behind me and step onto the pile of denim. My bare feet can't feel any protruding surfaces, which means they're empty. I step off and pick them up while he turns to face me.

Fuck, that means my ticket is in the shower.

I throw the jeans at him and he catches them. Making my way to the singular chair in the room, I sit down and look at him. I can feel the daggers shooting from my eyes and he does too, meekly taking a seat on the edge of the bed.

"Okay," I tell him, "get started."

Little does he know that the predator is about to become the prey.

CHAPTER 7

LOGAN

"**C**an I at least put a shirt on?" I ask Cassie with my hand gesturing towards the bathroom, where it lies on the floor.

She leans back in the chair and crosses her arm. "No."

Normally, I'd smile and make some quip about how if she wanted to go another round, all she has to do is ask, but these aren't normal conditions. Everything is so fucked up that I don't even know how to proceed. My mind immediately goes to Cassie as if she's my one and only priority. I stop and reflect on what I told her after she tried to hurt me in her fit of anger.

Everything.

I told her she means everything to me and that was enough to get her back. Will it be enough to keep her? I try to scan through any number of ways to make her stay. My bounty hunter's mind is working in overdrive to find the solution, the divine move that will get me everything. I sit on the bed, almost struck dumb by the simplest and only move that I had left.

I have to tell her the truth, all of it.

It's the riskiest move of all, but it also promises the highest reward. She'll stay. She'll stay and be with me. Everything else is inconsequential compared to that. What I want right now at this moment is for her to stay, choosing to stay, for me.

"My name is Logan Howard," I tell Cassie and her eyes narrow. Showing my palms, I say, "I swear, no more lies. That is my real legal name."

Her eyes go back to their normal state. Score one for me. Take small victories where you can.

"Alright, Logan Howard, what do you want to tell me?" she inquires while kicking one leg over the other.

Crossed knees and crossed arms, fuck, I've got my work cut out for me. I rake a hand through my hair to get it out of my face and take a deep breath. I've never told someone my story, ever. I've kept it hidden for so long because it's my shield. It protects me in a way, never having to risk getting hurt or caring too much, like my mother did. She wouldn't be proud of how I've handled my life since, being the lone wolf that I am. I don't want to be alone anymore.

"I guess I'll start at the very beginning, but there'll be some werewolf politics that are a little confusing," I say, meeting Cassie's gaze with mine, only to find ice waiting for me.

"I'm sure I'll be able to keep up," she retorts.

My face doesn't even try to smile, knowing that I'm on a tightrope that could snap at any moment.

"My mom's name was Alina Howard. She was adopted by non-supernaturals and things were great. But then she turned sixteen. That's when werewolves start to get acquainted with their wolf and the shift. During a full moon one night, she shifted into her wolf and her parents didn't know what to do. Her dad was a hunter and tried to shoot her. He missed and that's when she ran out into the night. When it was over, she knew she couldn't go back, not when she herself didn't understand what was going on. She made a choice to learn what she could and survive.

Cassie's silent as she watches me closely, and I have no idea whether she believes me. Whether making myself this vulnerable is going to pay off.

"Eventually, after a couple of years, she stumbled onto a pack, the Dark Thorn pack. They took pity on her after hearing about her troubles and brought her in. Even though she was an outsider and an omega, some happiness was coming back into her life. She learned about the history of werewolves and how we survive, learning what it means to be a part of the pack. That's when she met him..." I trail off, squeezing my hands till the knuckles go white. The thought of even saying his name, sharing what he did, sends my blood into a boil. I feel the scraping of the wolf within thirsting for that fucker's blood and I have to work to remain calm.

"She met him? Him, who?" Cassie's voice pierces the fog of rage billowing inside me. I release my hands and give a look in her direction, noticing her legs are uncrossed. Progress.

"That's when she met Silas. Apparently, he was charming, handsome, young and strong. My mom thought that they were developing a relationship. They had fun until she realized she was pregnant. Silas was ambitious, he knew that one way or another he would become the Alpha of the pack, even though he was only to be second in command. When the old Alpha died and his son was positioned to take on leadership of the pack, Silas challenged the new Alpha."

"Is this the werewolf politics you mentioned? Why would an Alpha have to accept the challenge?" Cassie asks, unfolding her arms and scooching ever so slightly away from the back of the chair and towards me.

"The role of the Alpha is to demonstrate strength. A strong Alpha means a strong pack. Him refusing a challenge is a sign of weakness, sowing seeds of doubt about his ability to lead. Silas knew this and he knew his opponent—they'd grown up together. Silas killed him even after the challenge was over and the victor decided. With the ruthless killing of his closest friend, he was the Alpha he always wanted. My mother was taken aback by the killing but knew that she would be a true part of the pack, the mate to the Alpha.

"She was so excited to tell him that she was pregnant but he got mad. See, my mother wasn't from a family in the pack. She had no history and was unknown and thus unwanted by Silas. He needed to think about taking a mate with a better pedigree, someone to better secure his place as the Alpha. He couldn't have a bastard-wolf roaming around, he would have to take care of it. So he made the smart move." I pause again, a lump choking the words back and water blurring the rim of my vision. I look down at my feet and bring a finger to wipe both eyes before finishing the tale.

"He cast her out. Said that she'd lied to the pack and was actually a spy from a rival pack. He painted her as some villain who had taken advantage of their hospitality. Even though they all knew, they stood by while she was forced back into the wilderness, leaving the second family she'd ever known. Eventually, she had me and promised to show me love like she was never shown. But she got sick, it can happen with someone in her... condition. She died and I've been scraping by ever since." I look up at Cassie and I see that she's sitting on the edge of the seat, leaning closer, listening intently.

"So how does all this lead to you and me?" she asks, looking at me with a questioning look, needing to know the answer.

I sigh knowing that this will be the part that will be the hardest for her to digest. "My mom waited till the end of her life to reveal the real identity of my dad, she used to just refer to him as 'My father or Dad'. When I found out, I swore on her death that I would kill Silas to get revenge. The problem is that I'm like my mom, a lone wolf and no history, so I had to build one. I became a bounty hunter to survive and to make a name for myself. Everything I did from the day my mom died was to get to Silas. He hired me to collect an innocent girl who had stumbled into the woods and saw something she shouldn't have. She got away but left something behind."

I reach into the small pocket within my jeans and pull out the necklace, dangling it in front of her. Cassie's hand flies instinctively to her throat, feeling a phantom imprint of the object that was a part of her. She shoots up from her seat and rips the necklace away from my hand, examining it in the light to ensure it's really hers. She starts to pace, holding the necklace in her closed fist, close to her chest.

"Not only were you sent to *collect* me for that crazy werewolf in the woods, but it turns out he's your father, who you've been set on killing ever since your mother died," she stops, her back to me. She turns around slowly meeting my gaze, understanding in her eyes. "I was going to be your ticket in. I was going to be the sacrificial lamb to get you close to Silas, close enough to kill him, to get your revenge... I think I'm going to be sick." The back of her free hand covers her mouth as she runs to the bathroom, sliding the door shut, locking me on the outside. The faucet is the first thing I hear; the sound of rushing water drowning out any other sounds from my wolf hearing.

"Cassie, it's true. You were just the tool to get my final revenge, but then I found you. I knew I needed to stay by your side but, everything changed when we slept together." I speak to the door, raising my volume so I know she can hear me. "I promise you that I don't want to hurt you or give you to Silas. This isn't a game for me anymore. For fuck's sake Cassie, I'm mated to you!"

I hit the door before leaning my back against it for support, sliding down till I'm sitting against it. The cold, hard feel of it against my naked back is nothing compared to the coldness I feel spreading in my chest. I'm going to lose her. I knew it was a possibility, but I held out hope that it wasn't going to happen. The faucet turns off and the door jostles in place, telling me that Cassie's sitting on the opposite side.

"What does mated mean?" I hear her voice beyond the door, quiet and unsure.

"It's when a wolf commits themselves to the one they are meant to be with forever. It can happen with humans, obviously, but with wolves it usually happens to both parties...but not always."

"Was that your mom's condition?"

I pause at her rebuttal. I have to confront the fear that's always plagued me whenever I heard about wolves becoming mated.

"Yes, she mated with Silas but he didn't mate with her. Being rejected, she could've bounced back from that. But being rejected by her mate, it was too much. She tried to keep going and did a great job raising me, but eventually her shattered heart won out. Don't you see Cassie? That is how I can make the promise that you mean everything to me, that you're safe and I won't turn you over to Silas. Because to do so would effectively be killing myself."

The door moves a little up and down. I look down to see three fingers poking out beside me. I move my own to lightly rest on them.

"How do you know? How do you know that you're mated to me?" Cassie asks. Her fingers feel like an anchor. After traversing the sea of my sad and lonely life, she brings calm and warmth.

"It's in our eyes, they glow. I can show you if you want."

Her fingers slip back behind the bathroom door and a silence grows between us.

CHAPTER 8

CASSIE

I don't know how long I've been sitting on the cool, dirty linoleum floor of Logan's...our...his...motel room bathroom.

It was just too much, all of it.

I suppress a laugh at the absurdity of it. What kind of lycanthropic Greek drama has my life become? I look down at my hands and the weight of my options literally caress the palms. In my left hand is my mother's necklace. Whatever the reason, Logan did reunite me with a part of my life I thought I would never have again. My Dad gave my mom this very necklace, a sign of how much he loved her. I bring my left hand above my head so that the necklace dangles in front of my nose. I guess in some twisted way, Logan gave it back for the same reason my dad gave it to my mom. My hand drops back to my side, collecting the necklace into its palm on the way down.

What am I supposed to do?

I make sure that whatever I do, I think it through silently. I don't want Logan to hear with that stupid werewolf hearing. What does it say about me that the only guy that I feel that "magic, instant connection" with is a werewolf who was sent to kill me? My right hand squeezes the contents within it. The worn but smooth texture of the leather wallet forces my eyes to examine my second set of options.

The wallet and set of keys that were tucked away in the pocket of Logan's shirt feel heavier than they should. My first and only thought when we came back has been getting into the bathroom. I'm finally here and I'm even more confused. My heart breaks for the story of Logan's life and I understand why he wants to kill Silas. Silas deserves it, but is this just another trick, another ploy? Everything Logan's told me has been a lie since he first picked me up off the side of the road.

Yet the word that I have been avoiding comes dancing to the front of my mind.

Mated.

He says that he's mated to me. That seeing me hurt or leaving me would be the same as swallowing a bullet. His poor mother did the best she could, and it wasn't enough. No wonder Logan has been so laser focused on getting to Silas. That man destroyed the only woman who ever loved him. Well, the first woman to...

I stop immediately. My brain goes quiet at the craziness that had almost entered my thoughts. Except that's when a warmth spreads from my chest and my eyes close, a smile creeping across my lips.

I love Logan Howard.

It is just that simple. It should be too soon. I should be checking myself into the nearest psychiatric ward. But the truth could be printed in one of my medical texts, it's just as irrefutable.

I love him. I want to give him the love that he's been deprived of for so long. I want to show him that being mated isn't the death sentence as it was for his mother. I want him to feel fully alive and not just survive.

The door jostles as I get up from my spot on the floor, my thigh muscles spasming at the flow of fresh blood. My eyes find the mirror and then travel down to my hands one last time, ready to make my choice. One of the objects comes to rest down on the counter and I turn away from it. With my back straightening and my head held high, I stand ready to proceed forward. The lock clicks its release of the door and I open it.

Logan is sitting on the side of the bed, still shirtless, his hair mussed as if he's been threading his fingers through it. He looks up at me, fear and worry gleaming in his eyes. I walk towards him and he begins to get up but I wave a hand at him, telling him to stay sitting. I'm standing a mere few inches away from him. He's looking up at me with those dark eyes.

"Show me." I ask him. His eyes go wide at the request, surprised I'm making it. "You said you would show me. Please," I ask again.

His lashes flutter shut and I wait patiently. Logan opens them and my jaw drops at the beauty swirling in their depths. Even in the horrible fluorescent motel light, the glow and warmth of the gold shimmering along the irises is a beauty beyond comparison. A beauty that exists because of me. For me.

I know the moment that the golden hue fades from them that I made the right choice. I hold out my left hand and let the necklace drop into his view. He glances at the jewelry and I ask, "Can you put it on me?" A smile of excitement plays across his features and he lifts me up into his arms as he gets to his feet. I squeal at my sudden departure from the ground and swing around in the air.

It's only when I'm placed back on the ground that Logan gently takes the necklace from my fingers and turns me around. The heat of his arms reaching around to my front is a shocking prelude to the cool and familiar metal of the necklace across my skin. My eyes close at the soft brushing of his fingertips against the back of my neck, securing the necklace. Every touch seems to have become a lightning storm, flashing through my body.

"Thank you Cassie. I promise to make you as happy as I can," Logan whispers into my ear before kissing a trail of heat from my earlobe to the top of my shoulder. I step away from him even though every fiber is screaming for me to melt into him. The look on his face when I turn around pains me deeply but I know what has to happen next. The next step before we can truly begin our lives.

"We have to come up with a plan, Logan. We can't have Silas looming over both of us."

Logan's shoulders slump forward a little. He didn't want to have to talk about Silas, especially after laying himself bare to me.

"Well, he wants you alive. So he can kill you, Cassie," he chokes on the latter end of the sentence, raking a hand through his hair.

"I'm assuming you already got some money when he hired you to find me. Why can't you just say that you lost me?"

"You don't get it. If I don't find and return you, there will be another bounty hunter to track you. He wants you alive so he can use you to demonstrate his power and authority. That even the risk of exposure is nothing that the great Silas Beaumont can't handle." Logan throws his hands up, his voice growing annoyed.

"So it's about exposure and the risk of a human knowing about werewolves..." I say, my brain starting to piece together the puzzle. I look back at him, the answer obvious. "Say you killed me."

Logan goes silent. He stares at me with wide eyes welling with tears, the mere thought being too much for him to even entertain. I rush to him and take his hands into mine, reassuring that I'm here and alive. "Think about it, Logan. If you tell Silas that you found me and agreed to meet, you can say that I tried to escape and got violent. One thing led to another and you had to kill me. But because you didn't want to risk being found out by the police, you decided to get rid of my body. You tell Silas that the job is done and return whatever money he already gave you. It's not as satisfying but it's what he ultimately wants. This way he gets to keep his money and go on knowing his pack and secret are safe."

Logan looks away from me while pressing his lips into a thin line. I can tell that he's thinking about my proposal, playing it through his mind.

"I think it could work if we're smart and play it just right," he says grudgingly. "There are some details we need to iron out but yeah, on the whole it could work."

I smile and nod that we're on the same page. The plan is going to be set into motion, starting now.

"Okay, I'll make contact," Logan says before lowering to lightly kiss me on the forehead.

He makes his way over to his bag and produces a cellphone. He brings it to his ear, and I can hear the dial tone ringing and ringing till the click on the other end. Something changes in Logan. His body becomes tauter, more alert, serious. "I have the girl. Arrange for a handoff thirty miles east of this location tomorrow night." He hangs up the phone and tosses it onto the chair I'd been sitting on.

He turns to me, the stiffness leaving his body, looking at me visibly relaxing him. He approaches me and I meet him, his hand cupping my face. Even though he's relaxed, I notice that there's a seriousness in his eyes. Tension builds up behind my neck and I start to wonder if something's wrong.

He closes his eyes and takes a deep breath. Is he taking in my scent? "Cassie, I've shown you I'm mated to you. You need to know if we make love, we complete the mating rite. I'll be bound to love you until the day I die. Is that what you want?"

I pause, taking in the words he just told me. He essentially just proposed the werewolf version of marriage. My hands come to rest on his shoulders and they tense a little at my touch. His gaze slides away.

He's nervous. He's unsure if I'm truly going to stay. My hands travel from his shoulders, down his muscular arms and finally hold his wrists.

"Logan, look at me," I command gently. "Yes, I want this. I want you. I wish my eyes could glow but you'll just have to take me at my human word. I'm yours, forever."

A smile of relief blossoms across his lips and his forehead comes to meet mine. We giggle at the intimacy of it, but somehow it just feels right and everything falls away. Any thoughts about our situation, what awaits us tomorrow night or Silas are a thousand miles away.

He releases my face and pulls me into him by the small of my back. My hands go to his beautiful dark hair, gripping tightly. I lean up to him, my lips searching for his and he meets them with hungry passion. The heat of his body burns into me, igniting every nerve with a firestorm. The ridges of his defined, muscular body prick at the desire pooling in my lower belly, even through the fabric cruelly separating us.

I need him, all of him. It's growing as quick as the pulse beneath my neck. My quick fingers reach down and make fast work of the button on his jeans and the zipper. I smile between kisses at him marching his feet on the bottoms of the jeans till they slip down to the floor.

I'm spun around suddenly and the bottom of my t-shirt is hiked up and over my face, exposing my breasts. The tips of his fingers caress the back of my neck, moving my hair to one side, revealing the landing pad for his incoming kisses. I let out a soft moan as his hands find their way to my hips. They're rough and calloused but in this moment, the most gentle touch I've experienced.

My nipples tighten at the growing pleasure spreading through my body. The calloused palms travel up my hips, the bottoms of my ribs and curving around the front, cupping my breasts. A few haggard breaths betray the heat every graze elicits. He squeezes and releases one breast while his fingers rub and roll the nipple of the other. My back arches, backing my ass into him. I can feel the heat and hardness of his erection rubbing against the fabric of my shorts, and my eyes flutter closed as need pounds through my veins.

Logan switches tactics between my breasts. The tip of his tongue moves up from the trapezius muscle to the secret spot on my neck. He gently sucks while tracing unknown designs with his tongue on the skin. I can't hold back the scream that's building up.

My legs are going weak when I decide it's my turn. I want to give this man the same pleasure he's unleashing within me. I reach up to his hands, bringing their torture to a stop. I turn around gently, peeling them away. I meet his eyes and don't look away while I lower myself to my knees, the motel carpet tickling my sensitized skin. I open my mouth and lightly grip the base of his penis with my fingers, positioning him just right.

I take him into my mouth and I hear a throaty growl. My thighs clench at the sound, needing to pull him into me. I start to take him in a little deeper only to retreat to the very tip and then continue, working a little closer to the base each time. His legs quiver, a positive sign that he's enjoying the appetizer. A pulse shoots through my vagina, excited at the pleasure my mouth is having. His breathing is growing quicker, no doubt focusing on not coming yet. I pull back, giving him a little respite, my right fingers curling around the shaft just behind his head. His tip is taken once again into my mouth and I move my mouth and hand as a unit.

"Fuck!" Logan gasps. "Cassie, I need to be inside you."

I look up and he's breathing like he's barely hanging on by a thread. I relinquish my grip and stand up, pulling my shorts and panties down as I go.

We stand there before each other naked, physically and emotionally. Nothing between us like the last time, nothing holding us back. Our sweat-slicked bodies collide as we embrace, trading kisses, hands groping anything and everything. His chest hair tickling my nipples and his firm dick pressing up into my navel. A few awkward, stumbling steps later, we find ourselves on the bed and he lays me down.

He rubs his penis against my clitoris and electricity convulses through me, my toes curling at the sensitivity. A few seconds later, he slowly enters me, just the tip sliding in while he positions himself above me.

I find his eyes framed by strands of black hair. They aren't looking anywhere else but at me. I'm not going to have to get him to look at me like last time. He needs to look at me. I'm his mate and he is the promise of a happy life, regardless of circumstance. I reach up, touching my palm to his cheek. He smiles and turns to kiss the inside of my wrist before allowing me to guide him down to my lips. Just before he kisses me, he enters me slowly until he completely fills me.

Our lips meet and just like before, his hips start to thrust back and forth, finding the rhythm as my hips buck to meet his. We fall into that sensual dance of love-making, kisses and adoring glances trading between the two of us.

Logan picks up the tempo and the tension builds faster and faster, deep within me. He rears up, still delivering a quick thrust deep inside me. A hand finds its way to resting on my pubis area, his fingers fanning out and pushing down. My arms spread out of their own accord, clenching the sheet between my tightening fingers. I can feel the tip of his erection teasing against the spot he's pushing down. I don't think I can take much more until his thumb starts to play with my clit. The tension within me shatters. I let out a gasp of unbelievable pleasure. The quickening contraction within me proves to be too much for Logan. He lets out an equally loud groan as I feel him finish inside of me.

He slowly pulls out, his body still shaking a little. I lick my lips before trying to catch my breath, savoring the wave peaking within me. Labored breathing and feeling the bed dip under his body betrays his position next to me, my hands rest delicately on my chest. Eventually, the wave breaks into oblivion and I turn to face him. He's looking at me, traces of the gold hue fading from his eyes.

"I'm going to have to get used to that…" I begin, but he cuts me off.

"I love you, Cassie."

I take a sharp breath, surprised at the directness of his confession. The reality is that we're about to attempt something recklessly stupid and dangerously risky, but what for if not for love? I lie here still reeling from the amazing sex and deep down I know that I feel it too. He didn't have to say it, the golden glow in his eyes was enough but he wants to. He wants me to know for as long as we're together.

So I do the only thing a girl can in this situation. I lean over, kiss him gently on the lips before I whisper. "I love you too, Logan."

He pulls me into his arms and we sleep.

We both know reality is coming at us, whether we like it or not.

But for now, we have each other, and the impossible love that was never meant to spark.

CHAPTER 9

LOGAN

The long road stretches out in front of me, my headlights illuminating the emptiness of it. If only my mind was equally empty. I'm on my way to meet with Silas and execute the plan that Cassie and I came up with.

We're going to be free of him.

Still, my mind is distracted, the one thing I never allow it to be when I'm working. This is going to be the most dangerous mission I've ever attempted. Cassie told me what happened to the last guy who failed Silas, which started this whole mess in the first place. All because Silas was searching for someone.

This morning we learned that her car is fixed and ready to go and that gives us an extra piece to work with. She has cash, a car and a burner phone with her. If I don't call the number, she'll know that I'm dead. I made her promise me she won't wait. To leave and start her new life.

I look to see the envelope that Silas had given me such a short time ago. It feels like another lifetime ago. I didn't know anything except for surviving and thinking only of my revenge. And then came Cassie. She's my touchstone. The example of what people should be and how they should love.

The sweet thoughts I'm thinking of my mate vanish as I see the bald, mountain of a man who is Silas's right-hand lackey. He's standing on the side of the road, no car near him. Strange. I slow down and pull off onto the grassy shoulder of the road, killing the engine and snuffing out the lights. The entire scenery plunges into darkness, save for the light of the full moon. With the envelope in hand, I get out of my car, lock it behind me and approach the mountain. His gaze meets mine and the familiar heat of werewolves seeing each other flashes through me.

"Where's the girl?" he asks.

I stand in front of him and give him the stink eye. "I'm sorry, is your name Silas? Do I work for you?"

Cassie is rubbing off on me quicker than I thought she would. The mountain doesn't betray any emotion. With a simple turn on his heels, he enters the thicket of trees off the side of the road. I take a deep breath, steeling myself for entering the wolf den.

We walk through the thicket and glide over the floor of the woods, not a single stick snaps beneath us or a rustle of branches betrays our approach. I'm impressed that the mountain can move quietly given his size. It's a telling sign to the skill of the wolf within him. Finally, we come to a clearing. Silas is there waiting for us, five others positioned around him. Six, actually, a meek boy in the back almost escaping my notice. He looks away from my gaze, timid in a way I can't understand right now.

I walk towards Silas, feeling the mountain covering my six and any hope of an escape. The reason for him leading becomes clear to me. It was a demonstration and a warning not to run. He can catch me and I'd never even hear him coming. I almost smile at the power move, except I feel the heat of Silas looking at me.

I stand there and it's completely different from the last time we were face to face.

The hatred that was begging, no, demanding I rip off his fucking head is diminished. I don't think it will ever go away. It will always be a part of me and who I am, but it no longer defines me. For too long, I've given this bastard too much power over my life. He's been pulling my strings and directing my path without even trying or caring. Cassie is the reason everything has changed. I don't want revenge anymore. I just want to be done with him for good and be with her. She's my redemption and the hope my mom had for me, even at the end.

Her final words play in my mind. *Don't be a lone wolf forever baby, find someone you love and who will love you back, as fully as the Wolf Moon.*

Don't worry Mom, I finally have her.

"Where's the bitch?" Silas asks, breaking the silence between us.

"There was a complication," I tell him, short and to the point.

"What kind of complication?"

I swallow before I respond. I need to remain calm, not give him any sign of worry. "While we were stopped so she could take a piss, she decided she'd try to and run. I caught her, of course, but the bitch stole my gun from my bag. I tried to wrestle it away from her, but it went off. She shot herself in the fucking stomach, bled out in less than a minute." I keep my voice as even as I possibly can. I've rehearsed this line over and over till it felt like breathing. The thought of Cassie dying in my arms is disconnected from it.

"Where's the body?" Silas looks at me as if he knows I'm lying.

"I didn't want to risk the police or anyone else finding her. So...I buried her. Don't worry, deep enough that no one is going to find her. But she's dead, so the risk of exposure is gone." I stretch out my hand with the envelope in it. "You wanted her alive, so here's your money back."

Silas takes the envelope and examines the inside of it, pausing as he reaches in. "And the necklace?"

It takes all of my will and strength not to have a physical response to the question. "I gave it back to her as a sign of trust but she had it on when she died, buried with her."

Silas smiles when he turns to his lackeys behind him, one of them taking the envelope before he returns his gaze to me. He laughs and the marrow in my bones chills to ice.

Something is wrong.

Something is terribly wrong.

"Boy, do you think that I'm stupid? You think you can pull a fast one over me? I am the Alpha of the Black Thorn pack, the strong and powerful Silas Beaumont. Nothing gets by me." He brings his fingers to his lips and lets out a whistle that pierces the quiet trees.

Two more men emerge from the side of the woods and my heart races at what I see. They have Cassie, wrists tied together and a cloth gagged in her mouth. My body tightens, muscles readying themselves to save my mate but two meaty arms, muscles firm as stone, wrap around me. The force pushes the air out of my lungs. The mountain has me in his grasp.

"Cassie! Don't you fucking touch her, Silas. Don't you fucking dare," I scream at Silas, glancing between his evil smile and Cassie's wide, wet eyes.

"Now, I'm no doctor but she don't look too dead to me."

"How? I only called you last night. No way you had someone already near us. I would've smelled them or felt their gaze."

It isn't adding up. No one was tailing me. No werewolf got within a mile of me and Cassie.

Silas stretches his arm out and half turns to the boy at the back. The one who looks as unwilling to be there as I am. Silas snaps his fingers and the boy shifts with his clothes on into a Shar Pei. The Shar Pei that submitted to my wolf form when Cassie discovered the truth. The dog shifts back into his human form, readjusting his clothes.

"Who knew mutts and half-breeds could come in handy? See, as a weredog or pathetic shifter, whatever you wanna call him, everything about him is diminished. That means no heat, no strong scent, not even the hint that he isn't just a stupid mut. Thanks, Billy Boy."

Silas turns to face me square on, approaching me while I'm trapped in this stronghold. He closes the distance and stops just before me. His nostrils dilate, allowing the scents of me to whirl into his nose. His eyes widen and a grin that would make the devil squirm dances across his features. "You dumb little cub. You got yourself some nice pussy and decided it's worth throwing away all that money? Possibly your life?"

Silas turns his predatory gaze to Cassie.

"Well, if it's that good...I might just have to try some for myself."

CHAPTER 10

CASSIE

The threat that Silas just made hangs in the air. Logan's eyes stay on me and I can see the horror in them. I can see it because the same icy fear is coursing through my veins.

I try to wiggle out of the hands of my captors, but their grips are just too strong. I recognize them from the night I saw Silas kill that man in the park. It seems like a completely different life and I guess it was. I've had it with life altering events throwing me about like a hot potato. I scream through the gag in my mouth, leaning towards where Logan is being restrained. He struggles to get free but only flinches as his captor increases his hold.

Silas lets out a laugh and claps his hands together, rubbing them with ferocious excitement. "She's got spirit. I like them spunky. It makes the moment they submit even sweeter. Tommy, why don't you go ahead and let this bitch have her say."

The man to the right of me, Tommy, reaches around with one hand and undoes the knot of the gag. The crumpled piece of cloth goes slack and I push it out of my mouth. Even though my dry mouth is quickly threatening to silence me, I'm able to voice a single word.

"Run," I scream, forcing all the fear that's constricting my heart into the command.

The echo of my plea dies within the thicket of the trees. Silas smiles and walks over to me. The grips holding onto me tighten, making sure I behave myself in front of their Alpha. He's only a foot away from me but I can smell the whiskey on his breath. A hand comes to the side of my head, twisting a lock of my hair between his fingers.

"I prefer you with blonde hair but that's alright. I'm sure the carpets are still in the original color," Silas chuckles and the men holding me join him.

I collect the spit that's been flooding my mouth and launch it right into Silas's face. I don't even see him move, but I feel it. The force in which he slaps me across the face threatens to snap my head off my spine. Stars dance across my field of vision and the taste of metallic notes and salt splash across my tongue. My eyes squeeze shut as pain ricochets through my skull.

"I will fucking kill you, you son of a bitch."

Logan's threats are the first thing I hear but then a dead silence follows them. With my vision returning to me and the blood seeping out of my mouth, I look to see the cause of the silence. Everyone, even myself, is looking at Logan. His eyes shine golden, blazing in the light of the moon above us.

Silas is in front of him in a few seconds with incredible speed. He grabs Logan's face around his chin, examining the golden glow. Logan resists, but eventually has to look upon him.

Silas whistles and nods for a moment before releasing Logan and stepping back. "It was dictated long ago that no other werewolf shall lie with another's mate. I tend to uphold that tradition, even for a lone wolf." I'm stunned thinking about how he probably slept with plenty of women after casting out Logan's mother. "But..."

I stop breathing, hating that word.

"You have done me wrong, pup, and as a lone wolf, I am within my right to seek retribution. To make sure that you know that no one is above the Black Thorn Pack. I will kill your mate and you shall walk away with your life."

My lungs burn for air but I can't give it to them. It's the smart move. It's the right move. I've known I was dead since that night in the park. At least this way, my death can mean something. It will mean that Logan can live on, maybe find another mate one day. He can live and finally experience the love I could have given him.

I finally inhale, deep and true, accepting this fate.

Silas angles his head. "It's too bad, really. You found her fast. Faster than any bounty hunter I've used before. I could've used you to find what I've really been searching for all these years."

The memory of what the murdered wolf said just before he died slam through me.

"I can still find him, Alpha. I just need another chance. Some more time."

Silas has been looking for his heir. For Logan!

The irony is bittersweet. The death I witnessed was his fury that Logan couldn't be found. And then he hired his own son to find me.

All that anger and vengeance has brought us to this moment.

One that I'm glad I could be part of, in a sad, twisted way. Maybe this was what I was meant to do. I'm giving Logan his freedom.

"No," he says resolutely. "Have the mountain wolf release

me. I'm not going to run." He pauses, looking over to me before continuing, "No more running."

My heart races as the gold fades from his eyes. "Logan, please, just leave. Live. Your mom would want you to live," I plead.

Sobs escape between a few of the words. The trickles from my eyes betray how scared I am for him, the man, no, the wolf that I love.

"It's okay, Cassie," he tells me before looking back to Silas. "Silas Beaumont, as the Alpha of the Black Thorn pack, I challenge you."

Silas takes a step back with a chuckle. "You ain't in my pack, boy. Why would I accept?"

The grip of the men holding me loosens a little. The mountain of man holding Logan releases him.

"Because if an Alpha is challenged by *any* werewolf, they must accept or lose favor with their pack. After all, you said you were one for tradition." Logan explains to Silas and the men who were holding me also release me. I hold my breath. It's a smart move. A masterful play that corners Silas in front of his pack.

A dangerous one.

Silas is vibrating with fury as he pulls out a gun, pointing it directly at Logan, ripping a shudder down my spine. "You think that you're smart, fucker? I don't have to do anything you say. I'm the fucking Alpha," Silas shouts, trying desperately to take back some of his power.

Logan doesn't even flinch. In fact, he looks away from Silas and addresses the pack gathered around. "Is this the mighty Alpha of the Black Thorn pack? A wolf who relies on a man's weapon to exert his dominance? A wolf who threatens to kill another's mate, rather than accept a proper challenge?" He turns back to Silas, his lip curling. "Guess it's not that surprising, seeing how he can't even make an heir. Three women you've taken as lovers and you're just shooting blanks. How much of an Alpha can someone be if they can't even get their bitches pregnant?"

The members of the pack glance at each other, finding the truth in Logan's words.

"He's a scared child. That is who your Alpha is. A child who bullies people into doing the things he wants. He doesn't have any real power. Just a happy trigger finger and a limp dick. Is this the kind of Alpha you want to be leading you?" Logan turns his back to Silas, looking at the other members of the pack.

It seems I'm the only one looking at Silas. His chest rising and puffing as anger heats him up from the inside. He throws the gun to the ground and rips off his shirt before launching at Logan. In midair, the manic man shifts into a wolf, leaving his jeans airborne.

Everything slows down, like when Logan shifted in front of me. I only have a few seconds to give my wolf a fighting chance.

Just before the jeans tumble to the ground, a final warning escapes my trembling lips.

"Logan!"

CHAPTER 11
LOGAN

The hairs on the back of my neck stand straight up when I hear Cassie scream my name. The snarls are the second thing I register.

I only have a few seconds which isn't ideal, but my life is on the line. I shift, watching Silas soaring over my wolf body. I back step my hind legs out of my jeans and begin to paw at the shirt and jacket that constrain me. I hear the soft land of Silas and scramble faster, needing to see my attacker to defend myself. I pull myself free from the rest of my clothes and see Silas approaching me.

His wolf form is gray, just like mine, but I can't think about that now. He's baring his teeth. I snap once in his direction, showing my teeth as well. The deadlock hangs between us for what feels like hours. I know that he's sizing me up, trying to plan his attack. I think back to our first encounter and all the knowledge I've collected on him.

He's strong, always has been, and in his office his reflexes were fast.

He launches himself at me and I try to dodge, but the force of his head collides with my hips. I go down, surprised, but roll myself back to my paws, hopefully minimizing his chances for a second attack. We face each other again. There's no point in waiting. There isn't a magic move that will bring him down. The only way out of this is through.

I snap at him and growl deep within my throat telling him, *this is the night you die motherfucker.* We both jump towards each other, claws outstretched. The impact sounds across the clearing and heralds the violence of a wolf fight.

Silas nips hard at my shoulder, tearing out a tuft of fur. My hips swing around to try and bounce him off. After getting a feel for his location, I kick with one of my hind legs, claws tearing into his undercoat. We tumble in a heap of fur and snarls. I don't have time to yelp at the scratches and bites. I have to deliver as many attacks as Silas is giving.

That's when I feel it. The soft give of his underbelly beneath one of my claws. It's not as ideal as my teeth, but it will deal some serious damage. A cry of pain escapes Silas and I know that I've taken the advantage.

At least that's what I think until in some crazy maneuver, Silas has me on my stomach pinned with his forepaws and his mouth around my scruff. Usually, when a wolf is pinned like this, the wolf with the advantage is giving the loser a chance to withdraw. Not Silas though. His bite force increases and I yelp at the pain. Teeth are slowly sinking in and drawing blood.

I can't understand how I'm going to lose. This is all I've wanted.

Now that I'm here, what's stopping me? Is revenge not enough? I yelp again and that's when I see her, Cassie. Fear is coming off of her in waves; I can smell it clearly even among the blood and saliva. She doesn't deserve to see me die. No, she doesn't deserve to have me die. She deserves to live and to live with me. She deserves the love that I can give her.

That's when it all falls into place. Revenge isn't enough to fight for, but love is. The promise of the love that I've been missing since I was born, since my mom died, because of him. I position my hind legs squarely beneath me, and with a howl and all the love in my heart, I buck Silas. The pain of his jaw releasing my scruff and freeing me is excruciating, but it fades.

Love is fueling me now, and I know what my next move is. Silas charges and I charge back. He jumps into the air but I stay low to the ground. I wait until he's overhead. Everything slows down. I see the trail of blood along his underbelly. I shift back into my human form and plow my first right into the dead center of the injury. Silas cries out in pain and shifts back into human form while in midair. The leaves on the ground crunch as he crashes onto the cold ground. Hard. An exaggerated exhale escapes his lips along with all the air in his lungs.

I waste no time. I slide down to the ground, positioning myself against his back. I wrap my arms around his throat and get him into a tight chokehold. He squirms in my grip, his oxygen levels already depleted from the impact. Elbows and fist try to break free but the force behind them is fading quickly.

This is it. I can finally kill him.

I look around at the pack members watching and see trepidation in their eyes. Some of them are half turned away from the scene, not able to stomach it.

Stomach what?

They can't stomach me. They think I'll be just like him.

I take a deep breath and whisper into Silas's ear. "Accept defeat. Save face in the eyes of your pack. Tap out and it will be over. You will never have to see me and Cassie ever again."

He continues to struggle but his movements are slowing down. I tighten my grip just a little, hoping the shock will bring him to his senses.

"Submit," I yell, more for the pack than myself.

Taps in rapid succession rap on my forearm. I exhale a sigh

of relief, exhaustion starting to seep into my muscles. I push Silas away, his gasps for air music to my ears. Getting to my knees, I see the gun that he pulled on me, the metal of the handle glimmering in the moonlight under some leaves. There's the quick crunching of leaves, as if there's a scramble behind me. I'm about to get up and turn around when Cassie screams.

"Knife."

My hand reaches out and grabs the gun. I pivot half a rotation in my kneeling position and aim in front of me, pulling the trigger.

The forest goes quiet and silence hangs in the aftermath of the shot.

Tinnitus settles into my ears. I always hate using guns— murder on wolf hearing. I see the bullet shoot through Silas's chest, blood instantly blooming. A flower of death.. He stands still like a statue, his body not processing what's happened yet.

The knife he has raised falls from his grip as he stumbles backwards and collapses. My hearing returns to the sound of him gargling on the blood flooding his lungs. I move around to his side, kneeling down by him. His eyes look at me with utter fear, knowing that he's going to die. I bend down close to him so he can hear me. Cassie may make me a better man, but after tonight. Right now, I just want his last moments to be filled with regret.

"I'll tell you my name, Silas. My real name as a final gift to you. My name is Logan Howard. My mother was Alina Howard."

His eyes go wide and he tries to speak. All he can do is choke on the blood crawling up his windpipe.

"That's right, the woman who you turned away was the only one who gave you an heir. An heir who just beat and killed you. Rot in hell, Silas Beaumont."

The light fades from his eyes and although there's not the satisfaction I always assumed there would be, there's a strange peace. I'm free of him. Cassie is free of him. Our future now stretches before us, bright and beautiful.

I stand up and turn towards Cassie, who has tears staining her lovely cheeks. I drop the gun and stretch out a hand towards her. We're free.

She runs to me and I help untie the binds on her hands. With her hands free, she wraps her arms around my naked waist and pulls me in. Her lips find mine and we kiss as if it was the first time. The pain and blood from the fight are nonexistent when I'm in her arms and tasting her lips. My hands find her cheeks, holding her in place. She's the breath of air I need and always will. Eventually, the both of us need air and we rest our foreheads against each other.

"What happens now?" she asks.

I lace my fingers within hers. "We get to live happily ever after."

I turn towards the direction of the car, but Cassie tugs me to come back.

She's looking at the pack and they're all staring back at us. "Black Thorn Pack, your Alpha has been defeated. Will you accept Logan Howard as your new Alpha?"

I close the distance and whisper to her, "What are you doing?"

She turns to me with a proud smile on her face. "Logan, I can be a lot of things for you, but I'm never going to be a wolf. You need to be with other wolves, you need a pack. You're proven your strength and fairness. You would be a strong, honorable leader."

Her eyes say what she doesn't want to say out loud. "You don't have to be a lone wolf anymore."

I look at the rest of the pack and find they're waiting for me to speak. I stand up straight and speak from my heart. "If you will have me, I will be your new Alpha of the Black Thorn Pack. But I am not Silas. I will not operate with fear and the threat of death. I promise to be fair and help all of us be the best wolves we can be. If you don't wish to be part of my pack, you are free to leave. You will not have to look over your shoulder. Will you accept me?"

The shifter boy, Billie is the first to leave the scene. I want to tell him not to go, but I won't question his choice. A couple more wander off, but the rest stay.

To my surprise, the mountain wolf is the one who speaks first. "To Logan Howard, the new Alpha of the Black Thorn pack." He strips and shifts into his wolf form.

The others gather, following suit. When I'm the only wolf still in human form, the pack of wolves throw their heads back and howl up into the night sky, celebrating my new position as their Alpha.

I turn to Cassie. "I love you." It's a thank you as well, one from the deepest recesses of my heart, but I'm sure she got the subtext. She's a smart one.

"I love you too," she tells me and brings me down for another kiss.

The first of thousands I plan to give her.

FIVE YEARS LATER

The drive home is a great way to end the day. The trees along the winding dirt road are starting to lose their green, only to give way to the bright colors that promise autumn. The driver's window of my black Escalade rolls down, granting entrance to the whips of the downforce wind. The smell of crisp air mixed with molting wood dances along its wings. My eyes close for a few seconds, relaxed, knowing no other cars are around.

I open them again and readjust my grip on the steering wheel. It's been an interesting five years for this former bounty hunter and lone wolf. I'm coming home from working at the security firm I own and operate, Howard Security Solutions. The large corporation we signed on today just cemented the company's place as a reliable provider of high-quality security.

I surrendered control of the construction business back to the family from which Silas stole it from, only to find out that it had belonged to Mountain Wolf, Michael's family. I asked if it was alright if I used the money that Silas promised to start my own business and the pack didn't fight me. They were relieved to be moving in a new direction. Living on the edge of the wrong side of the law, whether they liked it or not, was wearing thin to those who wanted security and family. Turns out my company did that for much more than just my clients.

Cassie finished her final year of medical school and was matched into her dream residency in emergency medicine. That's the reason I'm coming home a little earlier than usual. She's expected at the hospital for the night shift. Rounding the corner, I see the little house we built and a beaming smile comes across my lips like it always does. I'm truly living the life I didn't know I always wanted.

The one his mother had wanted for me.

I pull up to the stairs leading up to the front door. Cassie is going to need the space to pull out of the garage. I grab my computer bag from the passenger seat and slings it over my shoulder before reaching into my pocket for the keys. The familiar click of the lock alerts my arrival to the someone waiting patiently behind it.

"Daddy," a screech of delight rings in my ears.

A little girl with bouncing golden curls framing her face runs towards me. I bend down and scoop her up into my arms, growling playfully. As I nuzzle into her face, she bends her head towards me, hoping to hide her sensitive neck against my growing stubble, laughing the whole time. I pull back and pretend that I'm going to drop her, keeping her safe and secure the whole time.

"Did you have a fun day with Mommy today, little pup?" I ask, wandering into the kitchen, thinking a cold beer would only make this moment better.

"Yeah I did, but mommy was silly. She peed her pants," little Alina says, laughing at the memory. I paused with my beer in hand, glancing at my mother's namesake, confused. She stares back, wondering why I'm not understanding.

"Mommy peed her pants," Alina repeats but my attention is

pulled from my little girl as I smell my mate approaching from behind the corner. She smells like normal except with something else. Something I only smelled the last time.

"Mommy didn't pee her pants. Hi honey, my water broke," Cassie informs me, rounding the corner and using the wall to steady her waddle.

I try to stay calm. I really do. But I clank my beer onto the kitchen island, rushing to be by her side, that werewolf speed slipping out a little bit. Alina squeals at the headrush as if it's a normal trick daddy does with her.

"Are you okay? Does the hospital know? What do we need to do?"

Cassie brings her hand to my cheek, smiling calmly. Alina puts her hand on my other cheek closest to her.

"Yes, I'm okay. The contractions are starting to get annoying, but not too close together. I called my parents. They're going to meet us at the hospital to take Leeny overnight. We'll figure the rest out after we get this little one out into the world." She stares down at her very pregnant belly.

I place a hand on the vessel housing my second child, getting ready to enter the world. Cassie brings her hand to rest on top of mine. Their family is about to grow again. How in the world did I get so lucky?

Their beautiful moment is broken by Alina squirming in his arms. Her demands to be put down fill our ears.

"My go bag is on the bed," Cassie says, shaking her head indulgently. "Can you go pick it up while Alina helps me to the car?"

I nod, my eyes back to feeling like a deer in headlights. I deposit Alina back onto the ground before heading towards the back of the house. Thanks to my were speed, I'm back as Cassie and Alina are still walking toward the front door. Between

Cassie's waddle and our daughter's four-year-old legs, it's as if they've just traversed an oval.

Alina leaves Cassie only for a moment to slip on her "pretty pink princess" shoes, securing the Velcro proudly. The pair rejoin hands and begin their slow and steady walk to my car as I hover behind them. After a few huffs and puffs, Cassie finally gets into the passenger seat.

"Fingers and toes, mama," Alina announces.

Cassie dramatically shows that her hands and feet are safe from getting stuck in the door. It's something we taught Alina only a couple of years ago, although it seems longer than that. Alina closes the door after seeing that Cassie is safe in her seat.

I join them and open the back passenger door. "Come on Leeny, buckle yourself in," I instruct her.

She crawls into her booster seat, working the buckles as soon as her butt is firmly planted. I dash around the car, depositing the go bag behind the driver's seat before getting behind the wheel.

"Everyone buckled up?" I ask, looking at Cassie, seeing the seatbelt across her chest.

"Buckled and ready," Alina sounds off, excitement in her voice.

I look at Cassie, holding out my hand. She places hers into it and we give each other a squeeze.

"Are you ready for another one?" I ask with a smile, tilting my head towards Alina.

"Are you kidding me, compared to when we first met?" Cassie laughs, the sound still directly connected to my heart strings five years later. "This is a breeze. Leeny, are you excited for a little brother or sister?" Cassie asks, releasing my hand as I put the car into reverse.

"Little brother," Alina corrects.

"We don't know, Leeny, but we'll find out." I tell my daughter as I drive past the same trees I saw only a few minutes ago. Do they really seem brighter somehow in the dying daylight?

"I know. He's gonna be a boy wolf."

Cassie and I exchange a look, humoring our little girl's prediction.

We drive off into the city, excited to meet the newest member of our pack.

Seven hours later, at 12:37 a.m., 7 pounds and 6 ounces and 22 inches tall, Logan Howard Junior joins the world.

A child who will only know the warmth and love of an Alpha werewolf and his mate.

Looking for more sexy alphas and satisfying romance?
Check out Ruthless Wolf, Book 1 in the Diamond Alpha trilogy!
Only 99 or FREE in Kindle Unlimited

RUTHLESS WOLF

I watched my entire pack get slaughtered. My family. My friends. My future mate. Ever since, revenge has been my sole focus.

Adeline is the daughter of the Alpha responsible for my loss.

I've been watching her, learning. She's sweet. Innocent. Their pack's weakness.

One I'm going to take advantage of.

Except the first night we officially meet, everything changes. The chemistry is undeniable. Overwhelming. Something I quickly don't want to live without.

Except to have Adeline in my life, I have to let the hatred go. Turns out it can't coexist with the sweet forever she promises.

When my life has been defined by vengeance, I'm not sure that's possible.

The Forever Mates world is one of possessive, protective Alphas, steamy, satisfying romance, and the redeeming power of finding your forever mate. Expect addictive stories, sizzling chemistry, and sigh-worthy happily ever afters.

Only 99c or FREE in Kindle Unlimited!

GRAB YOUR COPY HERE
https://mybook.to/RuthlessWolfTM

WANT TO STAY IN TOUCH?

I mostly stay in contact with wonderful readers such as yourself through email. I send a fun, exciting newsletter once or twice a month to let you know of release days (which means more sexy supernatural time for you!) or to share relevant updates.

I also love to send sneaky snippets of upcoming books, early reveals of covers, and share other great reads.

SIGN UP HERE

I'd love to see you over there.
Tala :)

ALSO BY TALA MOORE

BLACK DIAMOND ALPHA

Ruthless Wolf

Rogue Wolf

Redeemed Wolf

COMING SOON!

SILVER MOON ALPHA

Forbidden Wolf

Forsaken Wolf

Forever Wolf

COMING SOON!

RED RIVER ALPHA

Enchanted Wolf

Enticed Wolf

Eternal Wolf

ABOUT THE AUTHOR

Tala Moore loves all things paranormal and romance. Give her possessive alpha males, sassy heroines, and a love that refuses to be denied, and she's set for as long as she can disappear from the world (which is never as long as she'd like!).

Driven to create the same swoon-worthy experience for others, she pens the Forever Mates story world. Dive in and discover her penchant for unforgettable characters, steamy romance, and a HEA that will stay with you long after the story is finished.

www.ingramcontent.com/pod-product-compliance
Lightning Source LLC
Chambersburg PA
CBHW020413150626
46554CB00013B/908